The Coral Tree

Ruskin Bond is known for his signature simplistic and witty writing style. He is the author of several bestselling short stories, novellas, collections, essays and children's books; and has contributed a number of poems and articles to various magazines and anthologies. At the age of twenty-three, he won the prestigious John Llewellyn Rhys Prize for his first novel, *The Room on the Roof*. He was also the recipient of the Padma Shri in 1999, Lifetime Achievement Award by the Delhi Government in 2012, and the Padma Bhushan in 2014.

Born in 1934, Ruskin Bond grew up in Jamnagar, Shimla, New Delhi and Dehradun. Apart from three years in the UK, he has spent all his life in India, and now lives in Landour, Mussoorie, with his adopted family.

RUSKIN BOND

The Coral Tree

RUPA

Published by
Rupa Publications India Pvt. Ltd 2018
7/16, Ansari Road, Daryaganj
New Delhi 110002

Sales centres:
Bengaluru Chennai
Hyderabad Jaipur Kathmandu
Kolkata Mumbai Prayagraj

Copyright © Ruskin Bond 2018

This is a work of fiction. Names, characters, places and incidents are either the product of the author's imagination or are used fictitiously and any resemblance to any actual person, living or dead, events or locales is entirely coincidental.

All rights reserved.
No part of this publication may be reproduced, transmitted, or stored in a retrieval system, in any form or by any means, electronic, mechanical, photocopying, recording or otherwise, without the prior permission of the publisher.

P-ISBN: 978-93-5304-046-8
E-ISBN: 978-93-5304-047-5

Ninth impression 2024

10 9

The moral right of the author has been asserted.

Printed in India

This book is sold subject to the condition that it shall not, by way of trade or otherwise, be lent, resold, hired out, or otherwise circulated, without the publisher's prior consent, in any form of binding or cover other than that in which it is published.

CONTENTS

Introduction	vii
Children of India	1
The Four Feathers	7
Pret in the House	13
Goodbye, Miss Mackenzie	18
The Tiger-King's Gift	24
The School among the Pines	35
Uncle Ken's Rumble in the Jungle	59
The Street of Lost Homes	65
The Tunnel	70
A Special Tree	78
Getting Granny's Glasses	85
Tremors in the Night	96
The Room of Many Colours	99
The Coral Tree	124

INTRODUCTION

My oldest memories are of my father and me living in a palace. Now don't mistake us for royals. My father was a teacher who ran a small school in a palace for the royal children. The pay wasn't much, but we had a palace to live in, the latest 1938 model Hillman to drive about in, and a number of servants. In those days, of course, everyone had servants (although the servants did not have any!). Ayah was our own; but the cook, the bearer, the gardener, and the bhisti were all provided by the State. Some days I sat in the schoolroom with the other children (who were all much older than me), sometimes I remained in the house with Ayah, sometimes I followed the gardener about the spacious garden. I was about seven and that was possibly the best time I've had.

I often think of my father while writing, if it hadn't been for him I probably wouldn't be here enjoying the luxury of the title 'Writer on the Hill'. It was he who introduced me to writing. I think of my father as a friend, because he gave me much companionship, so much of his time, even when he was desperately ill. When I lost him, I retreated to my island, living in my own head most of the time. From that loneliness, came the stories about trees and mountains, the people I knew while growing up, and life in the small towns of Dehra and Simla.

In this collection I've put together some of my stories that have my favourite characters—old Miss Mackenzie, my Uncle Ken, Granny and Mani, the four feathers and their tricks and plans, Hassan the baker, Bina and Prakash, and many more. In my stories these characters have led humble but meaningful lives—their tales running deeper than those of the rich and famous. For, happiness is found in simple things; as was said by Paramahansa Yogananda, 'Be as simple as you can be; you will be astonished to see how uncomplicated and happy your life can become.'

Ruskin Bond

CHILDREN OF INDIA

They pass me everyday, on their way to school—boys and girls from the surrounding villages and the outskirts of the hill station. There are no school buses plying for these children: they walk.

For many of them, it's a very long walk to school.

Ranbir, who is ten, has to climb the mountain from his village, four miles distant and 2,000 feet below the town level. He comes in all weathers, wearing the same pair of cheap shoes until they have almost fallen apart.

Ranbir is a cheerful soul. He waves to me whenever he sees me at my window. Sometimes he brings me cucumbers from his father's field. I pay him for the cucumbers; he uses the money for books or for small things needed at home.

Many of the children are like Ranbir—poor, but slightly better off than what their parents were at the same age. They cannot attend the expensive residential and private schools that abound here, but must go to the government-aided schools with only basic facilities. Not many of their parents managed to go to school. They spent their lives working in the fields or delivering milk in the hill station. The lucky ones got into the army. Perhaps Ranbir will do something different when he grows up.

He has yet to see a train but he sees planes flying over the mountains almost every day.

'How far can a plane go?' he asks.

'All over the world,' I tell him. 'Thousands of miles in a day. You can go almost anywhere.'

'I'll go round the world one day,' he vows. 'I'll buy a plane and go everywhere!'

And maybe he will. He has a determined chin and a defiant look in his eye.

The following lines in my journal were put down for my own inspiration or encouragement, but they will do for any determined young person:

> We get out of life what we bring to it. There is not a dream which may not come true if we have the energy which determines our own fate. We can always get what we want if we will it intensely enough... So few people succeed greatly because so few people conceive a great end, working towards it without giving up. We all know that the man who works steadily for money gets rich; the man who works day and night for fame or power reaches his goal. And those who work for deeper, more spiritual achievements will find them too. It may come when we no longer have any use for it, but if we have been willing it long enough, it will come!

◆

Up to a few years ago, very few girls in the hills or in the villages of India went to school. They helped in the home until they were old enough to be married, which wasn't very old. But there are now just as many girls as there are boys going to school.

Bindra is something of an extrovert—a confident fourteen year old who chatters away as she hurries down the road with her companions. Her father is a forest guard and knows me quite well: I meet him on my walks through the deodar woods behind Landour. And I had grown used to seeing Bindra almost every day. When she did not put in an appearance for a week, I asked her brother if anything was wrong.

'Oh, nothing,' he says, 'she is helping my mother cut grass. Soon the monsoon will end and the grass will dry up. So we cut it now and store it for the cows in winter.'

'And why aren't you cutting grass too?'

'Oh, I have a cricket match today,' he says, and hurries away to join his teammates. Unlike his sister, he puts pleasure before work!

Cricket, once the game of the elite, has become the game of the masses. On any holiday, in any part of this vast country, groups of boys can be seen making their way to the nearest field, or open patch of land, with bat, ball and any other cricketing gear that they can cobble together. Watching some of them play, I am amazed at the quality of talent, at the finesse with which they bat or bowl. Some of the local teams are as good, if not better, than any from the private schools, where there are better facilities. But the boys from these poor or lower middle class families will never get the exposure that is necessary to bring them to the attention of those who select state or national teams. They will never get near enough to the men of influence and power. They must continue to play for the love of the game, or watch their more fortunate heroes' exploits on television.

♦

As winter approaches and the days grow shorter, those children who live far away must quicken their pace in order to get home before dark. Ranbir and his friends find that darkness has fallen before they are halfway home.

'What is the time, Uncle?' he asks, as he trudges up the steep road past Ivy Cottage.

One gets used to being called 'Uncle' by almost every boy or girl one meets. I wonder how the custom began. Perhaps it has its origins in the folktale about the tiger who refrained from pouncing on you if you called him 'uncle'. Tigers don't eat their relatives! Or do they? The ploy may not work if the tiger happens to be a tigress. Would you call her 'Aunty' as she (or your teacher!) descends on you?

It's dark at six and by then, Ranbir likes to be out of the deodar forest and on the open road to the village. The moon and the stars and the village lights are sufficient, but not in the forest, where it is dark even during the day. And the silent flitting of bats and flying-foxes, and the eerie hoot of an owl, can be a little disconcerting for the hardiest of children. Once Ranbir and the other boys were chased by a bear.

When he told me about it, I said, 'Well, now we know you can run faster then a bear!'

'Yes, but you have to run downhill when chased by a bear.' He spoke as one having long experience of escaping from bears. 'They run much faster uphill!'

'I'll remember that,' I said, 'thanks for the advice.' And I don't suppose calling a bear 'Uncle' would help.

Usually Ranbir has the company of other boys, and they sing most of the way, for loud singing by small boys will silence owls and frighten away the forest demons. One of them plays a flute, and flute music in the mountains is always enchanting.

◆

Not only in the hills, but all over India, children are constantly making their way to and from school, in conditions that range from dust storms in the Rajasthan desert to blizzards in Ladakh and Kashmir. In the larger towns and cities, there are school buses, but in remote rural areas getting to school can pose a problem.

Most children are more than equal to any obstacles that may arise. Like those youngsters in the Ganjam district of Orissa. In the absence of a bridge, they swim or wade across the Dhanei river everyday in order to reach their school. I have a picture of them in my scrapbook. Holding books or satchels aloft in one hand, they do the breast stroke or dog paddle with the other; or form a chain and help each other across.

Wherever you go in India, you will find children helping out with the family's source of livelihood, whether it be drying fish on the Malabar Coast, or gathering saffron buds in Kashmir, or grazing camels or cattle in a village in Rajasthan or Gujarat.

Only the more fortunate can afford to send their children to English medium private or 'public' schools, and those children really are fortunate, for some of these institutions are excellent schools, as good, and often better, than their counterparts in Britain or USA. Whether it's in Ajmer or Bangalore, New Delhi or Chandigarh, Kanpur or Kolkata, the best schools set very high standards. The growth of a prosperous middle class has led to an ever-increasing demand for quality education. But as private schools proliferate, standards suffer too, and many parents must settle for the second-rate.

The great majority of our children still attend schools ran by the state or municipality. These vary from the good to the bad to the ugly, depending on how they are run and where they are situated. A classroom without windows, or with a roof that lets in the monsoon rain, is not uncommon. Even so, children from different communities learn to live and grow together. Hardship makes brothers of us all.

The census tells us that two in every five of the population is in the age group of five to fifteen. Almost half our population is on the way to school!

And here I stand at my window, watching some of them pass by—boys and girls, big and small, some scruffy, some smart, some mischievous, some serious, but all *going* somewhere—hopefully towards a better future.

THE FOUR FEATHERS

Our school dormitory was a very long room with about thirty beds, fifteen on either side of the room. This was good for pillow fights. Class V would take on class VII (the two senior classes in our Prep-school) and there would be plenty of space for leaping, struggling small boys, pillows flying, feathers flying, until there was a cry of 'Here comes Fishy!' or 'Here comes Olly!' and either Mr Fisher, the headmaster, or Mr Oliver, the senior master, would come striding in, cane in hand, to put an end to the general mayhem. Pillow fights were allowed, up to a point; nobody got hurt. But parents sometimes complained if, at the end of the term, a boy came home with a pillow devoid of cotton-wool or feathers.

In that last year at Prep-school in Simla, there were four of us who were close friends—Bimal, whose home was in Bombay; Riaz, who came from Lahore; Brian, who hailed from Vellore; and your narrator, who lived wherever his father (then in the Air Force) was posted.

We called ourselves 'four feathers'—the feathers signifying that we were companions in adventure, comrades in arms, knights of the round table, etc. Bimal adopted a peacock's feather as his emblem; he was always a bit showy. Riaz chose a falcon's feather—although we couldn't find one. Brian and I were at first offered crow's feathers, but we protested vigorously and threatened a walk-out. Finally, I settled for a parrot's feather (taken from Mr Fisher's pet parrot), and Brian found a woodpecker's, which suited him, as he was always knocking things about.

Bimal was all thin legs and arms, so light and frisky that at times he seemed to be walking on air. We called him 'Bambi', after the delicate little deer in the Disney film. Riaz, on the other hand, was a sturdy boy, good at games but not very studious; but always good-natured, always smiling. Brian was a dark, good-looking boy from the south; he was just a little spoilt—hated being given out in a cricket match and would refuse to leave the crease!—but he was affectionate and a loyal friend. I was the 'scribe'—good at inventing stories in order to get out of scrapes—but hopeless at sums, my highest marks being 22 out of 100.

On Sunday afternoons, when there were no classes or organized games, we were allowed to roam about on the hillside below the school. The four feathers would laze about on the short summer grass, sharing the occasional food parcel from home, reading comics (sometimes a book), and making plans for the long winter holidays. My father, who collected everything from stamps to sea-shells to butterflies, had given me a butterfly-net and urged me to try and catch a rare species which, he said, was found only near Chotta Simla. He described it as a large purple butterfly with yellow and black borders on its wings. A 'Purple Emperor', I think it was called. As I wasn't very good at identifying butterflies, I would chase anything that happened to flit across the school grounds, usually ending up with common 'red admirals', 'clouded yellows', or 'cabbage whites'. But that 'Purple Emperor'—that rare specimen being sought by collectors the world over—proved elusive. I would have to seek my fortune in some other line of endeavour.

One day, scrambling about among the rocks and thorny bushes below the school, I almost fell over a small bundle lying in the shade of a young spruce tree. On taking a closer look, I discovered that the bundle was really a baby, wrapped up in a tattered old blanket.

'Feathers, feathers!' I called, 'Come here and look. A baby's been left here!'

The feathers joined me, and we all stared down at the infant, who was fast asleep.

'Who would leave a baby on the hillside?' asked Bimal of no one in particular.

'Someone who doesn't want it,' said Brian.

'And hoped some good people would come along and keep it,' said Riaz.

'A panther might have come along instead,' I said. 'Can't leave it here.'

'Well, we'll just have to adopt it,' said Bimal.

'We can't adopt a baby,' said Brian.

'Why not?'

'We have to be married.'

'We don't.'

'Not us, you dope. The grown-ups who adopt babies.'

'Well, we can't just leave it here for grown-ups to come along,' I said.

'We don't even know if it's a boy or a girl,' said Riaz.

'Makes no difference. A baby's a baby. Let's take it back to school.'

'And keep it in the dormitory?'

'Of course not. Who's going to feed it? Babies need milk. We'll hand it over to Mrs Fisher. She doesn't have a baby.'

'Maybe she doesn't want one. Look, it's beginning to cry. Let's hurry!'

Riaz picked up the wide-awake and crying baby and gave it to Bimal who gave it to Brian who gave it to me. The four feathers marched up the hill to school with a very noisy baby.

'Now it has done potty in the blanket,' I complained, 'and some of it is on my shirt.'

'Never mind,' said Bimal. 'It's in a good cause. You're a Boy Scout, remember. You're supposed to help people in distress.'

The headmaster and his wife were in their drawing-room, enjoying their afternoon tea and cakes. We trudged in, and Bimal announced, 'We've got something for Mrs Fisher.'

Mrs Fisher took a look at the bundle in my arms and let out a shriek. 'What have you brought here, Bond?'

'A baby ma'am. I think it's a girl. Do you want to adopt it?'

Mrs Fisher threw up her arms in consternation, and turned to her husband. 'What are we to do, Frank? These boys are impossible. They've picked up someone's child!'

'We'll have to inform the police,' said Mr Fisher, reaching for the telephone, 'we can't have lost babies in the school.'

Just then there was a commotion outside, and a wild-eyed woman, her clothes disheveled, entered at the front door accompanied by several men-folk from one of the villages. She ran towards us, crying out, 'My baby, my baby! *Mera bachcha*! You've stolen my baby!'

'We found it on the hillside,' I stammered.

'That's right,' said Brian. 'Finders keepers!'

'Quiet, Adams,' said Mr Fisher, holding up his hand for order and addressing the villagers in a friendly manner. 'These boys found the baby alone on the hillside and brought it here before—before—'

'Before the hyaenas got it,' I put in.

'Quite right, Bond. And why did you leave your child alone?' he asked the woman.

'I put her down for five minutes so that I could climb the plum tree and collect the plums. When I came down, the baby was gone! But I could hear it crying up on the hill. I called the men-folk and we came here looking for it.'

'Well, here's your baby,' I said, thrusting it into her arms. By then I was glad to be rid of it! 'Look after it properly in future.'

'Kidnapper!' she screamed at me.

Mr Fisher succeeded in mollifying the villagers. 'These boys are good Scouts,' he told them. 'It's their business to help people.'

'Scout Laws Number Three, Sir,' I added. 'To be useful and helpful.'

And then the headmaster turned the tables on the villagers. 'By the way, these plum trees belong to the school. So do the peaches and apricots. Now I know why they've been disappearing so fast!'

The villagers, a little chastened, went their way. Mr Fisher reached for his cane. From the way he fondled it I knew he was itching to use it on our bottoms.

'No, Frank,' said Mrs Fisher, intervening on our behalf. 'It was really very sweet of them to look after that baby. And look at Bond—he's got baby-goo all over his clothes.'

'So he has. Go and take a bath, all of you. And what are you grinning about, Bond?' asked Mr Fisher.

'Scout Law Number Eight, Sir. A Scout smiles and whistles under all difficulties.'

And so ended the first adventure of the four feathers.

PRET IN THE HOUSE

It was Grandmother who decided that we must move to another house. And it was all because of a *pret*, a mischievous ghost, who had been making life intolerable for everyone.

In India, prets usually live in peepul trees, and that's where our Pret first had his abode—in the branches of an old peepul which had grown through the compound wall and had spread into the garden, on our side, and over the road, on the other side.

For many years, the Pret had lived there quite happily, without bothering anyone in the house. I suppose the traffic on the road had kept him fully occupied. Sometimes, when a tonga was passing, he would frighten the pony and, as a result, the little pony-cart would go reeling off the road. Occasionally he would get into the engine of a car or bus, which would soon afterwards have a breakdown. And he liked to knock the sola-topis off the heads of sahibs, who would curse and wonder how a breeze had sprung up so suddenly, only to die down again just as quickly. Although the Pret could make himself felt, and sometimes heard, he was invisible to the human eye.

At night, people avoided walking beneath the peepul tree. It was said that if you yawned beneath the tree, the Pret would jump down your throat and ruin your digestion. Grandmother's tailor, Jaspal, who never had anything ready on time, blamed the Pret for all his troubles. Once, when yawning, Jaspal had forgotten to snap his fingers in front of his mouth—always mandatory when yawning beneath peepul trees—and the Pret had got in without any difficulty. Since then, Jaspal had always been suffering from tummy upsets.

But it had left our family alone until, one day, the peepul tree had been cut down.

It was nobody's fault except, of course, that Grandfather had given the Public Works Department permission to cut the tree which had been standing on our land. They wanted to widen the road, and the tree and a bit of wall were in the way; so both had to go. In any case, not even a ghost can prevail against the PWD. But hardly a day had passed when we discovered that the Pret, deprived of his tree, had decided to take up residence in the bungalow. And since a good Pret must be bad in order to justify his existence, he was soon up to all sorts of mischief in the house.

He began by hiding Grandmother's spectacles whenever she took them off.

'I'm sure I put them down on the dressing-table,' she grumbled.

A little later they were found balanced precariously on the snout of a wild boar, whose stuffed and mounted head adorned the verandah wall. Being the only boy in the house, I was at first blamed for this prank; but a day or two later, when the spectacles disappeared again only to be discovered dangling from the wires of the parrot's cage, it was agreed that some other agency was at work.

Grandfather was the next to be troubled. He went into the garden one morning to find all his prized sweet-peas snipped off and lying on the ground.

Uncle Ken was the next to suffer. He was a heavy sleeper, and once he'd gone to bed, he hated being woken up. So when he came to the breakfast table looking bleary-eyed and miserable, we asked him if he wasn't feeling all right.

'I couldn't sleep a wink last night,' he complained. 'Every time I was about to fall asleep, the bedclothes would be pulled off the bed. I had to get up at least a dozen times to pick them off the floor.' He stared balefully at me. 'Where were you sleeping last night, young man?'

I had an alibi. 'In Grandfather's room,' I said.

'That's right,' said Grandfather. 'And I'm a light sleeper. I'd have woken up if he'd been sleep-walking.'

'It's that ghost from the peepul tree,' said Grandmother.

'It has moved into the house. First my spectacles, then the sweet-peas, and now Ken's bedclothes! What will it be up to next? I wonder!'

We did not have to wonder for long. There followed a series of disasters. Vases fell off tables, pictures came down the walls. Parrot feathers turned up in the teapot while the parrot himself let out indignant squawks in the middle of the night. Uncle Ken found a crow's nest in his bed, and on tossing it out of the window was attacked by two crows.

When Aunt Minnie came to stay, things got worse. The Pret seemed to take an immediate dislike to Aunt Minnie. She was a nervous, easily excitable person, just the right sort of prey for a spiteful ghost. Somehow her toothpaste got switched with a tube of Grandfather's shaving-cream, and when she appeared in the sitting-room, foaming at the mouth, we ran for our lives. Uncle Ken was shouting that she'd got rabies.

Two days later Aunt Minnie complained that she had been hit on the nose by a grapefruit, which had of its own accord taken a leap from the pantry shelf and hurtled across the room straight at her. A bruised and swollen nose testified to the attack. Aunt Minnie swore that life had been more peaceful in Upper Burma.

'We'll have to leave this house,' declared Grandmother.

'If we stay here much longer, both Ken and Minnie will have nervous breakdowns.'

'I thought Aunt Minnie broke down long ago,' I said.

'None of your cheek!' snapped Aunt Minnie.

'Anyway, I agree about changing the house,' I said breezily. 'I can't even do my homework. The ink-bottle is always empty.'

'There was ink in the soup last night.' That came from Grandfather.

And so, a few days and several disasters later, we began moving to a new house.

Two bullock-carts laden with furniture and heavy luggage were sent ahead. The roof of the old car was piled high with bags and kitchen utensils. Everyone squeezed into the car, and Grandfather took the driver's seat.

We were barely out of the gate when we heard a peculiar sound, as if someone was chuckling and talking to himself on the roof of the car.

'Is the parrot out there on the luggage-rack?' the query

came from Grandfather.

'No, he's in the cage on one of the bullock-carts,' said Grandmother.

Grandfather stopped the car, got out, and took a look at the roof.

'Nothing up there,' he said, getting in again and starting the engine. 'I'm sure I heard the parrot talking.'

Grandfather had driven some way up the road when the chuckling started again, followed by a squeaky little voice.

We all heard it. It was the Pret talking to itself.

'Let's go, let's go!' it squeaked gleefully. 'A new house. I can't wait to see it. What fun we're going to have!'

GOODBYE, MISS MACKENZIE

The Oaks, Holly Mount, The Parsonage, The Pines, Dumbarnie, Mackinnon's Hall, and Windermere. These are names of some of the old houses that still stand on the outskirts of one of the larger Indian hill stations. They were built over a hundred years ago by British settlers who sought relief from the searing heat of the plains. A few fell into decay and are now inhabited by wild cats, owls, goats, and the occasional mule-driver. Others survive.

Among these old mansions stands a neat, white-washed cottage, Mulberry Lodge. And in it lived an elderly British spinster named Miss Mackenzie. She was sprightly and wore old-fashioned but well-preserved dresses. Once a week, she walked up to town and bought butter, jam, soap and sometimes a bottle of eau-de-cologne.

Miss Mackenzie had lived there since her teens, before World War I. Her parents, brother, and sister were all dead. She had no relatives in India, and lived on a small pension and gift parcels sent by a childhood friend. She had few visitors—the local padre, the postman, the milkman. Like other lonely old people, she kept a pet, a large black cat with bright, yellow eyes.

In a small garden, she grew dahlias, chrysanthemums, gladioli and a few rare orchids. She knew a great deal about wild flowers, trees, birds, and insects. She never seriously studied them, but had an intimacy with all that grew and flourished around her.

It was September, and the rains were nearly over. Miss Mackenzie's African marigolds were blooming. She hoped the coming winter wouldn't be too severe because she found it increasingly difficult to bear the cold. One day, as she was puttering about in her garden, she saw a schoolboy plucking wild flowers on the slope above the cottage. 'What are you up to, young man?' she called.

Alarmed, the boy tried to dash up the hillside, but slipped on pine needles and slid down the slope into Miss Mackenzie's nasturtium bed. Finding no escape, he gave a bright smile and said, 'Good morning, Miss.'

'Good morning,' said Miss Mackenzie severely. 'Would you mind moving out of my flower bed?'

The boy stepped gingerly over the nasturtiums, and looked at Miss Mackenzie with appealing eyes.

'You ought to be in school,' she said. 'What are you doing here?'

'Picking flowers, Miss.' He held up a bunch of ferns and wild flowers.

'Oh,' Miss Mackenzie was disarmed. It had been a long time since she had seen a boy taking an interest in flowers.

'Do you like flowers?' she asked.

'Yes, Miss. I'm going to be a botan...a botanitist.'

'You mean a botanist?'

'Yes, Miss.'

'That's unusual. Do you know the names of these flowers?'

'This is a buttercup,' he said, showing her a small golden flower. 'But I don't know what this is,' he said, holding out a pale, pink flower with a heart-shaped leaf.

'It's a wild begonia,' said Miss Mackenzie. 'And that purple stuff is salvia. Do you have any books on flowers?'

'No, Miss.'

'Come in and I'll show you one.'

She led the boy into a small front room crowded with furniture, book vases and jam jars. He sat awkwardly on the edge of the chair. The cat jumped immediately on to his knees and settled down, purring softly.

'What's your name?' asked Miss Mackenzie, as she rummaged through her books.

'Anil, Miss.'

'And where do you live?'

'When school closes, I go to Delhi. My father has a business there.'

'Oh, and what's that?'

'Bulbs, Miss.'

'Flower bulbs?'

'No, electric bulbs.'

'Ah, here we are!' she said taking a heavy tome from the shelf. '*Flora Himaliensis*, published in 1892, and probably the only copy in India. This is a valuable book, Anil. No other naturalist has recorded as many wild Himalayan flowers. But there are still many plants unknown to the botanists who spend all their time at microscopes instead of in the mountains. Perhaps you'll do something about that one day.'

'Yes, Miss.'

She lit the stove and put the kettle on for tea. And then the old English lady and the small Indian boy sat side by side, absorbed in the book. Miss Mackenzie pointed out many flowers that grew around the hill station, while the boy made notes of their names and seasons.

'May I come again?' asked Anil, when finally he rose to go.

'If you like,' said Miss Mackenzie. 'But not during school hours. You mustn't miss your classes.'

After that, Anil visited Miss Mackenzie about once a week, and nearly always brought a wild flower for her to identify. She looked forward to the boy's visits. Sometimes when more than a week passed and he didn't come, she would grumble at the cat.

By the middle of October, with only a fortnight left before school closed, snow fell on the distant mountains. One peak stood high above the others, a white pinnacle against an azure sky. When the sun set, the peak turned from orange to pink to red.

'How high is that mountain?' asked Anil.

'It must be over 15,000 feet,' said Miss Mackenzie. 'I always wanted to go there, but there is no proper road. On the lower slopes, there'll be flowers that you don't get here: blue gentian, purple columbine.'

The day before school closed, Anil came to say goodbye. As he was about to leave, Miss Mackenzie thrust the *Flora Himaliensis* into his hands. 'It's a gift,' she said.

'But I'll be back next year, and I'll be able to look at it then,' he protested. 'Besides, it's so valuable!'

'That's why I'm giving it to you. Otherwise, it will fall into the hands of the junk dealers.'

'But, Miss...'

'Don't argue.'

The boy tucked the book under his arm, stood at attention, and said, 'Goodbye, Miss Mackenzie.' It was the first time he had spoken her name.

Strong winds soon brought rain and sleet, killing the flowers in the garden. The cat stayed indoors, curled up at the foot of the bed. Miss Mackenzie wrapped herself in old shawls and mufflers, but still felt cold. Her fingers grew so stiff that it took almost an hour to open a can of baked beans. Then it snowed, and for several days the milkman did not come.

Tired, she spent most of her time in bed. It was the warmest place. She kept a hot-water bottle against her back, and the cat kept her feet warm. She dreamed of spring and summer. In three months, the primroses would be out, and Anil would return.

One night the hot-water bottle burst, soaking the bed. The sun didn't shine for several days, and the blankets remained damp. Miss Mackenzie caught a chill and had to keep to her cold, uncomfortable bed.

A strong wind sprang up one night and blew the bedroom window open. Miss Mackenzie was too weak to get up and close it. The wind swept the rain and sleet into the room. The cat snuggled close to its mistress's body. Towards morning, the body lost its warmth, and the cat left the bed and started scratching about on the floor.

As sunlight streamed through the window, the milkman arrived. He poured some milk into the saucer on the doorstep, and the cat jumped down from the window-sill.

The milkman called out a greeting to Miss Mackenzie.

There was no answer. Knowing she was always up before sunrise, he poked his head in the open window and called again.

Miss Mackenzie did not answer. She had gone to the mountain, where the blue gentian and purple columbine grow.

THE TIGER-KING'S GIFT

Long ago in the days of the ancient Pandya kings of South India, a father and his two sons lived in a village near Madura. The father was an astrologer, but he had never become famous, and so was very poor. The elder son was called Chellan; the younger Gangan. When the time came for the father to put off his earthly body, he gave his few fields to Chellan, and a palm leaf with some words scratched on it to Gangan. These were the words that Gangan read:

>'From birth, poverty;
>For ten years, captivity;
>On the seashore, death.
>For a little while happiness shall follow.'

'This must be my fortune,' said Gangan to himself, 'and it doesn't seem to be much of a fortune. I must have done something terrible in a former birth. But I will go as a pilgrim to Papanasam and do penance. If I can expiate my sin, I may have better luck.'

His only possession was a water jar of hammered copper, which had belonged to his grandfather. He coiled a rope round the jar, in case he needed to draw water from a well. Then he put a little rice into a bundle, said farewell to his brother, and set out. As he journeyed he had to pass through a great forest. Soon he had eaten all his food and drunk all the water in his jar. In the heat of the day he became very thirsty.

At last he came to an old, disused well. As he looked down into it he could see that a winding stairway had once gone round it down to the water's edge, and that there had been four landing places at different heights down this stairway; so that those who wanted to fetch water might descend the stairway to the level of the water and fill their water-pots with ease, regardless of whether the well was full, or three-quarters full, or half full or only one quarter full.

Now the well was nearly empty. The stairway had fallen away. Gangan could not go down to fill his water-jar so he uncoiled his rope, tied his jar to it and slowly let it down. To his amazement, as it was going down past the first landing place, a huge striped paw shot out and caught it, and a growling voice called out: 'Oh Lord of Charity, have mercy! The stair is fallen. I die unless you save me! Fear me not. Though King of Tigers, I will not harm you.'

Gangan was terrified at hearing a tiger speak; but his kindness overcame his fear, and with a great effort, he pulled the beast up.

The Tiger-King—for it was indeed the Lord of all tigers bowed his head before Gangan, and reverently paced round him thrice from right to left as worshippers do round a shrine.

'Three days ago,' said the Tiger-King, 'a goldsmith passed by, and I followed him. In terror, he jumped down this well and fell on the fourth landing place below. He is there still. When I leaped after him I fell on the first landing place. On the third landing is a rat who jumped in when a great snake chased him.

And on the second landing, above the rat, is the snake who followed him. They will all clamour for you to draw them up.

'Free the snake, by all means. He will be grateful and will not harm you. Free the rat, if you will. But do not free the goldsmith, for he cannot be trusted. Should you free him, you will surely repent of your kindness. He will do you an injury for his own profit. But remember that I will help you whenever you need me.'

Then the Tiger-King bounded away into the forest.

Gangan had forgotten his thirst while he stood before the Tiger-King. Now he felt it more than before, and again let down his water-jar.

As it passed the second landing place on the ruined staircase, a huge snake darted out and twisted itself round the rope. 'Oh, Incarnation of Mercy, save me!' it hissed. 'Unless you help me, I must die here, for I cannot climb the sides of the well. Help me, and I will always serve you!'

Gangan's heart was again touched, and he drew up the snake. It glided round him as if he were a holy being. 'I am the Serpent-King,' it said. 'I was chasing a rat. It jumped into the well and fell on the third landing below. I followed, but fell on the second landing. Then the goldsmith leaped in and fell on the fourth landing place, while the tiger fell on the top landing. You saved the Tiger-King. You have saved me. You may save the rat, if you wish. But do not free the goldsmith. He is not to be trusted. He will harm you if you help him. But I will not forget you, and will come to your aid if you call upon me.'

Then the King of Snakes disappeared into the long grass of the forest.

Gangan let down his jar once more, eager to quench his

thirst. But as the jar passed the third landing, the rat leaped into it.

'After the Tiger-King, what is a rat?' said Gangan to himself, and pulled the jar up.

Like the tiger and the snake, the rat did reverence, and offered his services if ever they were needed. And like the tiger and the snake, he warned Gangan against the goldsmith. Then the Rat-King—for he was none other—ran off into a hole among the roots of a banyan tree.

By this time Gangan's thirst was becoming unbearable. He almost flung the water-jar down the well. But again the rope was seized, and Gangan heard the goldsmith beg piteously to be hauled up.

'Unless I pull him out of the well, I shall never get any water,' groaned Gangan. 'And after all, why not help the unfortunate man?' So with a great struggle—for he was a very fat goldsmith—Gangan got him out of the well and on to the grass beside him.

The goldsmith had much to say. But before listening to him, Gangan let his jar down into the well a fifth time. And then he drank till he was satisfied.

'Friend and deliverer!' cried the goldsmith. 'Don't believe what those beasts have said about me! I live in the holy city of Tenkasi, only a day's journey north of Papanasam. Come and visit me whenever you are there. I will show you that I am not an ungrateful man.' And he took leave of Gangan and went his way.

'From birth, poverty.'

Gangan resumed his pilgrimage, begging his way to Papanasam. There he stayed many weeks, performing all the ceremonies which pilgrims should perform, bathing at the waterfall, and watching the Brahmin priests feeding the fishes in the sacred stream. He visited other shrines, going as far as Cape Comorin, the southernmost tip of India, where he bathed in the sea. Then he came back through the jungles of Travancore.

He had started on his pilgrimage with his copper water-jar and nothing more. After months of wanderings, it was still the only thing he owned. The first prophecy on the palm leaf had already come true: 'From birth, poverty.'

During his wanderings Gangan had never once thought of the Tiger-King and the others, but as he walked wearily along in his rags, he saw a ruined well by the roadside, and it reminded him of his wonderful adventure. And just to see if the Tiger-King was genuine, he called out: 'Oh King of Tigers, let me see you!' No sooner had he spoken than the Tiger-King leaped out of the bushes, carrying in his mouth a glittering golden helmet, embedded with precious stones.

It was the helmet of King Pandya, the monarch of the land.

The King had been waylaid and killed by robbers, for the sake of the jewelled helmet; but they in turn had fallen prey to the tiger, who had walked away with the helmet.

Gangan of course knew nothing about all this, and when the Tiger-King laid the helmet at his feet, he stood stupefied at its splendour and his own good luck.

After the Tiger-King had left him, Gangan thought of the goldsmith. 'He will take the jewels out of the helmet, and I will sell some of them. Others I will take home.' So, he wrapped the helmet in a rag and made his way to Tenkasi.

In the Tenkasi bazaar he soon found the goldsmith's shop. When they had talked awhile, Gangan uncovered the golden helmet. The goldsmith—who knew its worth far better than

Gangan—gloated over it, and at once agreed to take out the jewels and sell a few so that Gangan might have some money to spend.

'Now let me examine this helmet at leisure,' said the goldsmith. 'You go to the shrines, worship, and come back. I will then tell you what your treasure is worth.'

Gangan went off to worship at the famous shrines of Tenkasi. And as soon as he had gone, the goldsmith went off to the local magistrate.

'Did not the herald of King Pandya's son come here only yesterday and announce that he would give half his kingdom to anyone who discovered his father's murderer?' he asked. 'Well, I have found the killer. He has brought the King's jewelled helmet to me this very day.'

The magistrate called his guards, and they all hurried to the goldsmith's shop and reached it just as Gangan returned from his tour of the temples.

'Here is the helmet!' exclaimed the goldsmith to the magistrate. 'And here is the villain who murdered the King to get it!'

The guards seized poor Gangan and marched him off to Madura, the capital of the Pandya kingdom, and brought him before the murdered King's son. When Gangan tried to explain about the Tiger-King, the goldsmith called him a liar, and the new King had him thrown into the death-cell, a deep, well-like pit, dug into the ground in a courtyard of the palace. The only entrance to it was a hole in the pavement of the courtyard. Here Gangan was left to die of hunger and thirst.

At first Gangan lay helpless where he had fallen. Then, looking around him, he found himself on a heap of bones, the bones of those who before him had died in the dungeon; and he was watched by an army of rats who were waiting to gnaw his dead body. He remembered how the Tiger-King had warned him against the goldsmith, and had promised help if ever it was needed.

'I need help now,' groaned Gangan, and shouted for the Tiger-King, the Snake-King, and the Rat-King.

For some time nothing happened. Then all the rats in the dungeon suddenly left him and began burrowing in a corner between some of the stones in the wall. Presently Gangan saw that the hole was quite large, and that many other rats were coming and going, working at the same tunnel. And then the Rat-King himself came through the little passage, and he was followed by the Snake-King, while a great roar from outside told Gangan that the Tiger-King was there.

'We cannot get you out of this place,' said the Snake-King. 'The walls are too strong. But the armies of the Rat-King will bring rice-cakes from the palace kitchens, and sweets from the shops in the bazaars, and rags soaked in water. They will not let you die. And from this day on the tigers and the snakes will slay tenfold, and the rats will destroy grain and cloth as never before. Before long the people will begin to complain. Then, when you hear anyone passing in front of your cell, shout: 'These disasters are the results of your Ruler's injustice! But I can save you from them!' At first they will pay no attention. But after some time they will take you out, and at your word we will stop the sacking and the slaughter. And then they will honour you.'

'For ten years, captivity.'

For ten years the tigers killed. The serpents struck. The

rats destroyed. And at last the people wailed, 'The gods are plaguing us.'

All the while Gangan cried out to those who came near his cell, declaring that he could save them; they thought he was a madman. So ten years passed, and the second prophecy on the palm leaf was fulfilled.

At last the Snake-King made his way into the palace and bit the King's only daughter. She was dead in a few minutes.

The King called for all the snake-charmers and offered half his kingdom to any one of them who would restore his daughter to life. None of them was able to do so. Then the King's servants remembered the cries of Gangan and remarked that there was a madman in the dungeons who kept insisting that he could bring an end to all their troubles. The King at once ordered the dungeon to be opened. Ladders were let down. Men descended and found Gangan, looking more like a ghost than a man. His hair had grown so long that none could see his face. The King did not remember him, but Gangan soon reminded the King of how he had condemned him without enquiry, on the word of the goldsmith.

The King grovelled in the dust before Gangan, begged forgiveness, and entreated him to restore the dead Princess to life.

'Bring me the body of the Princess,' said Gangan.

Then he called on the Tiger-King and the Snake-King to come and give life to the Princess. As soon as they entered the royal chamber, the Princess was restored to life.

Glad as they were to see the Princess alive, the King and his courtiers were filled with fear at the sight of the Tiger-King and the Snake-King. But the tiger and the snake hurt no one;

and at a second prayer from Gangan, they brought life to all those they had slain.

And when Gangan made a third petition, the Tiger, the Snake and the Rat-Kings ordered their subjects to stop pillaging the Pandya kingdom, so long as the King did no further injustice.

'Let us find that treacherous goldsmith and put him in the dungeon,' said the Tiger-King.

But Gangan wanted no vengeance. That very day he set out for his village to see his brother, Chellan, once more. But when he left the Pandya king's capital, he took the wrong road. After much wandering, he found himself on the sea-shore.

Now it happened that his brother was also making a journey in those parts, and it was their fate that they should meet by the sea. When Gangan saw his brother, his gladness was so sudden and so great that he fell down dead.

And so the third prophecy was fulfilled:

'On the sea-shore, death.'

Chellan, as he came along the shore road, had seen a half-ruined shrine of Pillaiyar, the elephant-headed God of good luck. Chellan was a very devout servant of Pillaiyar, and the day being a festival day, he felt it was his duty to worship the god. But it was also his duty to perform the funeral rites for his brother.

The sea-shore was lonely. There was no one to help him. It would take hours to collect fuel and driftwood enough for a funeral pyre. For a while Chellan did not know what to do, but at last he took up the body and carried it to Pillaiyar's temple.

Then he addressed the God. 'This is my brother's body,' he said. 'I am unclean because I have touched it. I must go and bathe in the sea. Then I will come and worship you, and afterwards I will burn my brother's body. Meanwhile, I leave it in your care.' Chellan left, and the God told his attendant Ganas (goblins) to watch over the body. These Ganas are inclined to be mischievous, and when the God wasn't looking, they gobbled up the body of Gangan.

When Chellan came back from bathing, he reverently worshipped Pillaiyar. He then looked for his brother's body. It was not to be found. Anxiously, he demanded it of the God. Pillaiyar called on his goblins to produce it. Terrified, they confessed to what they had done.

Chellan reproached the God for the misdeeds of his attendants. And Pillaiyar felt so much pity for him, that by his divine power he restored dead Gangan's body to Chellan, and brought Gangan to life again.

The two brothers then returned to King Pandya's capital, where Gangan married the Princess and became king when her father died.

And so the fourth prophecy was fulfilled:

'For a little while happiness shall follow.'

But there are wise men who say that the lines of the prophecy were wrongly read and understood, and that the whole should run:

'From birth, poverty;
For ten years, captivity;
On the sea-shore, death for a little while;
Happiness shall follow.'

It is the last two lines that are different. And this must be the correct version, because when happiness came to Gangan it was not 'for a little while'. When the Goddess of good fortune did arrive, she stayed in his palace for many, many years.

THE SCHOOL AMONG THE PINES

1

A leopard, lithe and sinewy, drank at the mountain stream, and then lay down on the grass to bask in the late February sunshine. Its tail twitched occasionally and the animal appeared to be sleeping. At the sound of distant voices it raised its head to listen, then stood up and leapt lightly over the boulders in the stream, disappearing among the trees on the opposite bank.

A minute or two later, three children came walking down the forest path. They were a girl and two boys, and they were singing in their local dialect an old song they had learnt from their grandparents.

'Five more miles to go!
We climb through rain and snow.
A river to cross...
A mountain to pass...
Now we've four more miles to go!'

Their school satchels looked new, their clothes had been washed and pressed. Their loud and cheerful singing startled a Spotted Forktail. The bird left its favourite rock in the stream and flew down the dark ravine.

'Well, we have only three more miles to go,' said the bigger boy, Prakash, who had been this way hundreds of times. 'But first we have to cross the stream.'

He was a sturdy twelve-year-old with eyes like raspberries and a mop of bushy hair that refused to settle down on his head. The girl and her younger brother were taking this path for the first time.

'I'm feeling tired, Bina,' said the little boy.

Bina smiled at him, and Prakash said, 'Don't worry, Sonu, you'll get used to the walk. There's plenty of time.' He glanced at the old watch he'd been given by his grandfather. It needed constant winding. 'We can rest here for five or six minutes.'

They sat down on a smooth boulder and watched the clear water of the shallow stream tumbling downhill. Bina examined the old watch on Prakash's wrist. The glass was badly scratched and she could barely make out the figures on the dial. 'Are you sure it still gives the right time?' she asked.

'Well, it loses five minutes every day, so I put it ten minutes forward at night. That means by morning it's quite accurate! Even our teacher, Mr Mani, asks me for the time. If he doesn't ask, I tell him! The clock in our classroom keeps stopping.'

They removed their shoes and let the cold mountain water run over their feet. Bina was the same age as Prakash. She had pink cheeks, soft brown eyes, and hair that was just beginning to lose its natural curls. Hers was a gentle face, but a determined little chin showed that she could be a strong person. Sonu, her younger brother, was ten. He was a thin boy who had been sickly as a child but was now beginning to fill out. Although he did not look very athletic, he could run like the wind.

Bina had been going to school in her own village of Koli, on the other side of the mountain. But it had been a Primary School, finishing at Class Five. Now, in order to study in the Sixth, she would have to walk several miles every day to Nauti, where there was a High School going up to the Eighth. It had been decided that Sonu would also shift to the new school, to give Bina company. Prakash, their neighbour in Koli, was already a pupil at the Nauti school. His mischievous nature, which sometimes got him into trouble, had resulted in his having to repeat a year.

But this didn't seem to bother him. 'What's the hurry?' he had told his indignant parents. 'You're not sending me to a foreign land when I finish school. And our cows aren't running away, are they?'

'You would prefer to look after the cows, wouldn't you?' asked Bina, as they got up to continue their walk.

'Oh, school's all right. Wait till you see old Mr Mani. He always gets our names mixed up, as well as the subjects he's supposed to be teaching. At out last lesson, instead of maths, he gave us a geography lesson!'

'More fun than maths,' said Bina.

'Yes, but there's a new teacher this year. She's very young, they say, just out of college. I wonder what she'll be like.'

Bina walked faster and Sonu had some trouble keeping up with them. She was excited about the new school and the prospect of different surroundings. She had seldom been outside her own village, with its small school and single ration shop. The day's routine never varied—helping her mother in the fields or with household tasks like fetching water from the spring or cutting grass and fodder for the cattle. Her father, who was a soldier, was away for nine months in the year and Sonu was still too small for the heavier tasks.

As they neared Nauti village, they were joined by other children coming from different directions. Even where there were no major roads, the mountains were full of little lanes and shortcuts. Like a game of snakes and ladders, these narrow paths zigzagged around the hills and villages, cutting through fields and crossing narrow ravines until they came together to form a fairly busy road along which mules, cattle and goats joined the throng.

Nauti was a fairly large village, and from here a broader but dustier road started for Tehri. There was a small bus, several trucks and (for part of the way) a road-roller. The road hadn't been completed because the heavy diesel roller couldn't take the steep climb to Nauti. It stood on the roadside halfway up the road from Tehri.

Prakash knew almost everyone in the area, and exchanged greetings and gossip with other children as well as with muleteers, bus drivers, milkmen and labourers working on the road. He loved telling everyone the time, even if they weren't interested.

'It's nine o'clock,' he would announce, glancing at his wrist. 'Isn't your bus leaving today?'

'Off with you!' the bus driver would respond, 'I'll leave when I'm ready.'

As the children approached Nauti, the small flat school buildings came into view on the outskirts of the village, fringed with a line of long-leaved pines. A small crowd had assembled on the playing field. Something unusual seemed to have happened. Prakash ran forward to see what it was all about. Bina and Sonu stood aside, waiting in a patch of sunlight near the boundary wall.

Prakash soon came running back to them. He was bubbling over with excitement.

'It's Mr Mani!' he gasped. 'He's disappeared! People are saying a leopard must have carried him off!'

2

Mr Mani wasn't really old. He was about fifty-five and was expected to retire soon. But for the children, adults over forty seemed ancient! And Mr Mani had always been a bit absent-minded, even as a young man.

He had gone out for his early morning walk, saying he'd be back by eight o'clock, in time to have his breakfast and be ready for class. He wasn't married, but his sister and her husband stayed with him. When it was past nine o'clock his sister presumed he'd stopped at a neighbour's house for breakfast (he loved tucking into other people's breakfast) and that he had gone on to school from there. But when the school bell rang at ten o'clock, and everyone but Mr Mani was present, questions were asked and guesses were made.

No one had seen him return from his walk and enquiries made in the village showed that he had not stopped at anyone's house. For Mr Mani to disappear was puzzling; for him to disappear without his breakfast was extraordinary.

Then a milkman returning from the next village said he had seen a leopard sitting on a rock on the outskirts of the pine forest. There had been talk of a cattle-killer in the valley, of leopards and other animals being displaced by the construction of a dam. But as yet no one had heard of a leopard attacking a man. Could Mr Mani have been its first victim? Someone found a strip of red cloth entangled in a blackberry bush and went running through the village showing it to everyone. Mr Mani had been known to wear red pyjamas. Surely, he had been seized and eaten! But where were his remains? And why had he been in his pyjamas?

Meanwhile, Bina and Sonu and the rest of the children had followed their teachers into the school playground. Feeling a little lost, Bina looked around for Prakash. She found herself facing a dark slender young woman wearing spectacles, who must have been in her early twenties—just a little too old to be another student. She had a kind, expressive face and she seemed a little concerned by all that had been happening.

Bina noticed that she had lovely hands; it was obvious that the new teacher hadn't milked cows or worked in the fields!

'You must be new here,' said the teacher, smiling at Bina. 'And is this your little brother?'

'Yes, we've come from Koli village. We were at school there.'

'It's a long walk from Koli. You didn't see any leopards, did you? Well, I'm new too. Are you in the Sixth class?'

'Sonu is in the Third. I'm in the Sixth.'

'Then I'm your new teacher. My name is Tania Ramola. Come along, let's see if we can settle down in our classroom.'

Mr Mani turned up at twelve o'clock, wondering what all the fuss was about. No, he snapped, he had not been attacked by a leopard; and yes, he had lost his pyjamas and would someone kindly return them to him?

'How did you lose your pyjamas, Sir?' asked Prakash.

'They were blown off the washing line!' snapped Mr Mani.

After much questioning, Mr Mani admitted that he had

gone further than he had intended, and that he had lost his way coming back. He had been a bit upset because the new teacher, a slip of a girl, had been given charge of the Sixth, while he was still with the Fifth, along with that troublesome boy Prakash, who kept on reminding him of the time! The headmaster had explained that as Mr Mani was due to retire at the end of the year, the school did not wish to burden him with a senior class. But Mr Mani looked upon the whole thing as a plot to get rid of him. He glowered at Miss Ramola whenever he passed her. And when she smiled back at him, he looked the other way!

Mr Mani had been getting even more absent-minded of late—putting on his shoes without his socks, wearing his homespun waistcoat inside out, mixing up people's names, and of course, eating other people's lunches and dinners. His sister had made a special mutton broth (pai) for the postmaster, who was down with 'flu' and had asked Mr Mani to take it over in a thermos. When the postmaster opened the thermos, he found only a few drops of broth at the bottom—Mr Mani had drunk the rest somewhere along the way.

When sometimes Mr Mani spoke of his coming retirement, it was to describe his plans for the small field he owned just behind the house. Right now, it was full of potatoes, which did not require much looking after; but he had plans for growing dahlias, roses, French beans, and other fruits and flowers.

The next time he visited Tehri, he promised himself, he would buy some dahlia bulbs and rose cuttings. The monsoon season would be a good time to put them down. And meanwhile, his potatoes were still flourishing.

3

Bina enjoyed her first day at the new school. She felt at ease with Miss Ramola, as did most of the boys and girls in her class. Tania Ramola had been to distant towns such as Delhi and Lucknow—places they had only read about—and it was said that she had a brother who was a pilot and flew planes all over the world. Perhaps he'd fly over Nauti someday!

Most of the children had, of course, seen planes flying overhead, but none of them had seen a ship, and only a few had been on a train. Tehri mountain was far from the railway and hundreds of miles from the sea. But they all knew about the big dam that was being built at Tehri, just forty miles away.

Bina, Sonu and Prakash had company for part of the way home, but gradually the other children went off in different directions. Once they had crossed the stream, they were on their own again.

It was a steep climb all the way back to their village. Prakash had a supply of peanuts which he shared with Bina and Sonu, and at a small spring they quenched their thirst.

When they were less than a mile from home, they met a postman who had finished his round of the villages in the area and was now returning to Nauti.

'Don't waste time along the way,' he told them. 'Try to get home before dark.'

'What's the hurry?' asked Prakash, glancing at his watch. 'It's only five o'clock.'

'There's a leopard around. I saw it this morning, not far from the stream. No one is sure how it got here. So don't take any chances. Get home early.'

'So there really is a leopard,' said Sonu.

They took his advice and walked faster, and Sonu forgot to complain about his aching feet.

They were home well before sunset.

There was a smell of cooking in the air and they were hungry.

'Cabbage and roti,' said Prakash gloomily. 'But I could eat anything today.' He stopped outside his small slate-roofed house, and Bina and Sonu waved him goodbye, then carried on across a couple of ploughed fields until they reached their small stone house.

'Stuffed tomatoes,' said Sonu, sniffing just outside the front door.

'And lemon pickle,' said Bina, who had helped cut, sun and salt the lemons a month previously.

Their mother was lighting the kitchen stove. They greeted her with great hugs and demands for an immediate dinner. She was a good cook who could make even the simplest of dishes taste delicious. Her favourite saying was, 'Home-made pai is better than chicken soup in Delhi,' and Bina and Sonu had to agree.

Electricity had yet to reach their village, and they took their meal by the light of a kerosene lamp. After the meal, Sonu settled down to do a little homework, while Bina stepped outside to look at the stars.

Across the fields, someone was playing a flute. 'It must be Prakash,' thought Bina. 'He always breaks off on the high notes.' But the flute music was simple and appealing, and she began singing softly to herself in the dark.

4

Mr Mani was having trouble with the porcupines. They had been getting into his garden at night and digging up and eating his potatoes. From his bedroom window—left open, now that the mild-April weather had arrived—he could listen to them enjoying the vegetables he had worked hard to grow. Scrunch, scrunch! *Katar, katar*, as their sharp teeth sliced through the largest and juiciest of potatoes. For Mr Mani, it was as though they were biting through his own flesh. And the sound of them digging industriously as they rooted up those healthy, leafy plants, made him tremble with rage and indignation. The unfairness of it all!

Yes, Mr Mani hated porcupines. He prayed for their destruction, their removal from the face of the earth. But, as his friends were quick to point out, 'Bhagwan protected porcupines too,' and in any case you could never see the creatures or catch them, they were completely nocturnal.

Mr Mani got out of bed every night, torch in one hand, a stout stick in the other, but as soon as he stepped into the garden the crunching and digging stopped and he was greeted by the most infuriating of silences. He would grope around in the dark, swinging wildly with the stick, but not a single porcupine was to be seen or heard. As soon as he was back in bed—the sounds would start all over again. Scrunch, scrunch, *katar, katar*...

Mr Mani came to his class tired and dishevelled, with rings beneath his eyes and a permanent frown on his face. It took some time for his pupils to discover the reason for his misery, but when they did, they felt sorry for their teacher and took to discussing ways and means of saving his potatoes from the porcupines.

It was Prakash who came up with the idea of a moat or waterditch. 'Porcupines don't like water,' he said knowledgeably.

'How do you know?' asked one of his friends.

'Throw water on one and see how it runs! They don't like getting their quills wet.'

There was no one who could disprove Prakash's theory, and the class fell in with the idea of building a moat, especially as it meant getting most of the day off.

'Anything to make Mr Mani happy,' said the headmaster, and the rest of the school watched with envy as the pupils of Class Five, armed with spades and shovels collected from all parts of the village, took up their positions around Mr Mani's potato field and began digging a ditch.

By evening the moat was ready, but it was still dry and the porcupines got in again that night and had a great feast.

'At this rate,' said Mr Mani gloomily 'there won't be any potatoes left to save.'

But next day Prakash and the other boys and girls managed to divert the water from a stream that flowed past the village. They had the satisfaction of watching it flow gently into the ditch. Everyone went home in a good mood. By nightfall, the ditch had overflowed, the potato field was flooded, and Mr Mani found himself trapped inside his house. But Prakash and his friends had won the day. The porcupines stayed away that night!

A month had passed, and wild violets, daisies and buttercups now sprinkled the hill slopes, and on her way to school Bina gathered enough to make a little posy. The bunch of flowers fitted easily into an old ink-well. Miss Ramola was delighted to find this little display in the middle of her desk.

'Who put these here?' she asked in surprise.

Bina kept quiet, and the rest of the class smiled secretively. After that, they took turns bringing flowers for the classroom.

On her long walks to school and home again, Bina became aware that April was the month of new leaves. The oak leaves were bright green above and silver beneath, and when they rippled in the breeze they were like clouds of silvery green. The path was strewn with old leaves, dry and crackly. Sonu loved kicking them around.

Clouds of white butterflies floated across the stream. Sonu was chasing a butterfly when he stumbled over something dark and repulsive. He went sprawling on the grass. When he got to his feet, he looked down at the remains of a small animal.

'Bina! Prakash! Come quickly!' he shouted.

It was part of a sheep, killed some days earlier by a much larger animal.

'Only a leopard could have done this,' said Prakash.

'Let's get away, then,' said Sonu. 'It might still be around!'

'No, there's nothing left to eat. The leopard will be hunting elsewhere by now. Perhaps it's moved on to the next valley.'

'Still, I'm frightened,' said Sonu. 'There might be more leopards!'

Bina took him by the hand. 'Leopards don't attack humans!' she said.

'They will, if they get a taste for people!' insisted Prakash.

'Well, this one hasn't attacked any people as yet,' said Bina, although she couldn't be sure. Hadn't there been rumours of a leopard attacking some workers near the dam? But she did not want Sonu to feel afraid, so she did not mention the story.

All she said was, 'It has probably come here because of all the activity near the dam.'

All the same, they hurried home. And for a few days, whenever they reached the stream, they crossed over very quickly, unwilling to linger too long at that lovely spot.

5

A few days later, a school party was on its way to Tehri to see the new dam that was being built.

Miss Ramola had arranged to take her class, and Mr Mani, not wishing to be left out, insisted on taking his class as well. That meant there were about fifty boys and girls taking part in the outing. The little bus could only take thirty. A friendly truck driver agreed to take some children if they were prepared to sit on sacks of potatoes. And Prakash persuaded the owner of the diesel-roller to turn it round and head it back to Tehri—with him and a couple of friends up on the driving seat.

Prakash's small group set off at sunrise, as they had to walk some distance in order to reach the stranded road-roller. The bus left at 9 a.m. with Miss Ramola and her class, and Mr Mani and some of his pupils. The truck was to follow later.

It was Bina's first visit to a large town and her first bus ride.

The sharp curves along the winding, downhill road made several children feel sick. The bus driver seemed to be in a tearing hurry. He took them along at rolling, rollicking speed, which made Bina feel quite giddy. She rested her head on her arms and refused to look out of the window. Hairpin bends and cliff edges, pine forests and snow-capped peaks, all swept past her, but she felt too ill to want to look at anything. It was just as well—those sudden drops, hundreds of feet to the valley below, were quite frightening. Bina began to wish that she hadn't come—or that she had joined Prakash on the road-roller instead!

Miss Ramola and Mr Mani didn't seem to notice the lurching and groaning of the old bus. They had made this journey many times. They were busy arguing about the advantages and disadvantages of large dams—an argument that was to continue on and off for much of the day; sometimes in Hindi, sometimes in English, sometimes in the local dialect!

Meanwhile, Prakash and his friends had reached the roller. The driver hadn't turned up, but they managed to reverse it and get it going in the direction of Tehri. They were soon overtaken by both the bus and the truck but kept moving along at a steady chug. Prakash spotted Bina at the window of the bus and waved cheerfully. She responded feebly.

Bina felt better when the road levelled out near Tehri. As they crossed an old bridge over the wide river, they were startled by a loud bang which made the bus shudder. A cloud of dust rose above the town.

'They're blasting the mountain,' said Miss Ramola.

'End of a mountain,' said Mr Mani mournfully.

While they were drinking cups of tea at the bus stop, waiting for the potato truck and the road-roller, Miss Ramola and Mr Mani continued their argument about the dam. Miss Ramola maintained that it would bring electric power and water for irrigation to large areas of the country, including the surrounding area. Mr Mani declared that it was a menace, as it was situated in an earthquake zone. There would be a terrible disaster if the dam burst! Bina found it all very confusing. And what about the animals in the area, she wondered, what would happen to them?

The argument was becoming quite heated when the potato truck arrived. There was no sign of the road-roller, so it was decided that Mr Mani should wait for Prakash and his friends while Miss Ramola's group went ahead.

Some eight or nine miles before Tehri the road-roller had broken down, and Prakash and his friends were forced to walk. They had not gone far, however, when a mule train came along—five or six mules that had been delivering sacks of grain in Nauti. A boy rode on the first mule, but the others had no loads.

'Can you give us a ride to Tehri?' called Prakash.

'Make yourselves comfortable,' said the boy.

There were no saddles, only gunny sacks strapped on to the mules with rope. They had a rough but jolly ride down to the Tehri bus stop. None of them had ever ridden mules; but they had saved at least an hour on the road.

Looking around the bus stop for the rest of the party, they could find no one from their school. And Mr Mani, who should have been waiting for them, had vanished.

6

Tania Ramola and her group had taken the steep road to the hill above Tehri. Half-an-hour's climbing brought them to a little plateau which overlooked the town, the river and the dam-site.

The earthworks for the dam were only just coming up, but a wide tunnel had been bored through the mountain to divert the river into another channel. Down below, the old town was still spread out across the valley and from a distance it looked quite charming and picturesque.

'Will the whole town be swallowed up by the waters of the dam?' asked Bina.

'Yes, all of it,' said Miss Ramola. 'The clock tower and the old palace. The long bazaar, and the temples, the schools and the jail, and hundreds of houses, for many miles up the valley. All those people will have to go—thousands of them! Of course, they'll be resettled elsewhere.'

'But the town's been here for hundreds of years,' said Bina. 'They were quite happy without the dam, weren't they?'

'I suppose they were. But the dam isn't just for them—it's for the millions who live further downstream, across the plains.'

'And it doesn't matter what happens to this place?'

'The local people will be given new homes, somewhere else.' Miss Ramola found herself on the defensive and decided to change the subject. 'Everyone must be hungry. It's time we had our lunch.'

Bina kept quiet. She didn't think the local people would want to go away. And it was a good thing, she mused, that there was only a small stream and not a big river running past her village. To be uprooted like this—a town and hundreds of villages—and put down somewhere on the hot, dusty plains—seemed to her unbearable.

'Well, I'm glad I don't live in Tehri,' she said.

She did not know it, but all the animals and most of the birds had already left the area. The leopard had been among them.

They walked through the colourful, crowded bazaar, where fruit-sellers did business beside silversmiths, and pavement vendors sold everything from umbrellas to glass bangles. Sparrows attacked sacks of grain, monkeys made off with bananas, and stray cows and dogs rummaged in refuse bins, but nobody took any notice. Music blared from radios. Buses blew their horns. Sonu bought a whistle to add to the general din, but Miss Ramola told him to put it away. Bina had kept ten rupees aside, and now she used it to buy a cotton head-scarf for her mother.

As they were about to enter a small restaurant for a meal, they were joined by Prakash and his companions; but of Mr Mani there was still no sign.

'He must have met one of his relatives,' said Prakash. 'He has relatives everywhere.'

After a simple meal of rice and lentils, they walked the length of the bazaar without seeing Mr Mani. At last, when they were about to give up the search, they saw him emerge from a by-lane, a large sack slung over his shoulder.

'Sir, where have you been?' asked Prakash. 'We have been looking for you everywhere.'

On Mr Mani's face was a look of triumph.

'Help me with this bag,' he said breathlessly.

'You've bought more potatoes, sir,' said Prakash.

'Not potatoes, boy. Dahlia bulbs!'

7

It was dark by the time they were all back in Nauti. Mr Mani had refused to be separated from his sack of dahlia bulbs, and had been forced to sit in the back of the truck with Prakash and most of the boys.

Bina did not feel so ill on the return journey. Going uphill was definitely better than going downhill! But by the time the bus reached Nauti it was too late for most of the children to walk back to the more distant villages. The boys were put up in different homes, while the girls were given beds in the school verandahh.

The night was warm and still. Large moths fluttered around the single bulb that lit the verandahh. Counting moths, Sonu soon fell asleep. But Bina stayed awake for some time, listening to the sounds of the night. A nightjar went *tonk-tonk* in the bushes, and somewhere in the forest an owl hooted softly. The sharp call of a barking deer travelled up the valley, from the direction of the stream. Jackals kept howling. It seemed that there were more of them than ever before.

Bina was not the only one to hear the barking deer. The leopard, stretched full length on a rocky ledge, heard it too. The leopard raised its head and then got up slowly. The deer was its natural prey. But there weren't many left, and that was why the leopard, robbed of its forest by the dam, had taken to attacking dogs and cattle near the villages.

As the cry of the barking deer sounded nearer, the leopard left its lookout point and moved swiftly through the shadows towards the stream.

8

In early June the hills were dry and dusty, and forest fires broke out, destroying shrubs and trees, killing birds and small animals. The resin in the pines made these trees burn more fiercely, and the wind would take sparks from the trees and carry them into the dry grass and leaves, so that new fires would spring up before the old ones had died out. Fortunately, Bina's village was not in the pine belt; the fires did not reach it. But Nauti was surrounded by a fire that raged for three days, and the children had to stay away from school.

And then, towards the end of June, the monsoon rains arrived and there was an end to forest fires. The monsoon lasts three months and the lower Himalayas would be drenched in rain, mist and cloud for the next three months.

The first rain arrived while Bina, Prakash and Sonu were returning home from school. Those first few drops on the dusty path made them cry out with excitement. Then the rain grew heavier and a wonderful aroma rose from the earth.

'The best smell in the world!' exclaimed Bina.

Everything suddenly came to life. The grass, the crops, the trees, the birds. Even the leaves of the trees glistened and looked new.

That first wet weekend, Bina and Sonu helped their mother plant beans, maize and cucumbers. Sometimes, when the rain was very heavy, they had to run indoors. Otherwise they worked in the rain, the soft mud clinging to their bare legs.

Prakash now owned a black dog with one ear up and one ear down. The dog ran around getting in everyone's way, barking at cows, goats, hens and humans, without frightening any of them. Prakash said it was a very clever dog, but no one else seemed to think so. Prakash also said it would protect the village from the leopard, but others said the dog would be the first to be taken—he'd run straight into the jaws of Mr Spots!

In Nauti, Tania Ramola was trying to find a dry spot in the quarters she'd been given. It was an old building and the roof was leaking in several places. Mugs and buckets were scattered about the floor in order to catch the drip.

Mr Mani had dug up all his potatoes and presented them to the friends and neighbours who had given him lunches and dinners. He was having the time of his life, planting dahlia bulbs all over his garden.

'I'll have a field of many-coloured dahlias!' he announced.

'Just wait till the end of August!'

'Watch out for those porcupines,' warned his sister. 'They eat dahlia bulbs too!'

Mr Mani made an inspection tour of his moat, no longer in flood, and found everything in good order. Prakash had done his job well.

Now, when the children crossed the stream, they found that the water-level had risen by about a foot. Small cascades had turned into waterfalls. Ferns had sprung up on the banks. Frogs chanted.

Prakash and his dog dashed across the stream. Bina and Sonu followed more cautiously. The current was much stronger now and the water was almost up to their knees. Once they had crossed the stream, they hurried along the path, anxious not to be caught in a sudden downpour.

By the time they reached school, each of them had two or three leeches clinging to their legs. They had to use salt to remove them. The leeches were the most troublesome part of the rainy season. Even the leopard did not like them. It could not lie in the long grass without getting leeches on its paws and face.

One day, when Bina, Prakash and Sonu were about to cross the stream they heard a low rumble, which grew louder every second. Looking up at the opposite hill, they saw several trees shudder, tilt outwards and begin to fall. Earth and rocks bulged out from the mountain, then came crashing down into the ravine.

'Landslide!' shouted Sonu.

'It's carried away the path,' said Bina. 'Don't go any further.'

There was a tremendous roar as more rocks, trees and

bushes fell away and crashed down the hillside.

Prakash's dog, who had gone ahead, came running back, tail between his legs.

They remained rooted to the spot until the rocks had stopped falling and the dust had settled. Birds circled the area, calling wildly. A frightened barking deer ran past them.

'We can't go to school now,' said Prakash. 'There's no way around.'

They turned and trudged home through the gathering mist.

In Koli, Prakash's parents had heard the roar of the landslide. They were setting out in search of the children when they saw them emerge from the mist, waving cheerfully.

9

They had to miss school for another three days, and Bina was afraid they might not be able to take their final exams. Although Prakash was not really troubled at the thought of missing exams, he did not like feeling helpless just because their path had been swept away. So he explored the hillside until he found a goat-track going around the mountain. It joined up with another path near Nauti. This made their walk longer by a mile, but Bina did not mind. It was much cooler now that the rains were in full swing.

The only trouble with the new route was that it passed close to the leopard's lair. The animal had made this area its own since being forced to leave the dam area.

One day Prakash's dog ran ahead of them, barking furiously. Then he ran back, whimpering.

'He's always running away from something,' observed Sonu. But a minute later he understood the reason for the dog's fear.

They rounded a bend and Sonu saw the leopard standing in their way. They were struck dumb—too terrified to run. It was a strong, sinewy creature. A low growl rose from its throat. It seemed ready to spring.

They stood perfectly still, afraid to move or say a word. And the leopard must have been equally surprised. It stared at them for a few seconds, then bounded across the path and into the oak forest.

Sonu was shaking. Bina could hear her heart hammering. Prakash could only stammer: 'Did you see the way he sprang? Wasn't he beautiful?'

He forgot to look at his watch for the rest of the day.

A few days later Sonu stopped and pointed to a large outcrop of rock on the next hill.

The leopard stood far above them, outlined against the sky. It looked strong, majestic. Standing beside it were two young cubs.

'Look at those little ones!' exclaimed Sonu.

'So it's a female, not a male,' said Prakash.

'That's why she was killing so often,' said Bina. 'She had to feed her cubs too.'

They remained still for several minutes, gazing up at the leopard and her cubs. The leopard family took no notice of them.

'She knows we are here,' said Prakash, 'but she doesn't care. She knows we won't harm them.'

'We are cubs too!' said Sonu.

'Yes,' said Bina. 'And there's still plenty of space for all of us. Even when the dam is ready there will still be room for leopards and humans.'

The school exams were over. The rains were nearly over too. The landslide had been cleared, and Bina, Prakash and Sonu were once again crossing the stream.

There was a chill in the air, for it was the end of September.

Prakash had learnt to play the flute quite well, and he played on the way to school and then again on the way home. As a result he did not look at his watch so often.

One morning they found a small crowd in front of Mr Mani's house.

'What could have happened?' wondered Bina. 'I hope he hasn't got lost again.'

'Maybe he's sick,' said Sonu.

'Maybe it's the porcupines,' said Prakash.

But it was none of these things.

Mr Mani's first dahlia was in bloom, and half the village had turned out to look at it! It was a huge red double dahlia, so heavy that it had to be supported with sticks. No one had ever seen such a magnificent flower!

Mr Mani was a happy man. And his mood only improved over the coming week, as more and more dahlias flowered—crimson, yellow, purple, mauve, white—button dahlias, pompom dahlias, spotted dahlias, striped dahlias... Mr Mani had them all! A dahlia even turned up on Tania Romola's desk—he got on quite well with her now—and another brightened up the headmaster's study.

A week later, on their way home—it was almost the last day of the school term—Bina, Prakash and Sonu talked about what they might do when they grew up.

'I think I'll become a teacher,' said Bina. 'I'll teach children about animals and birds, and trees and flowers.'

'Better than maths!' said Prakash.

'I'll be a pilot,' said Sonu. 'I want to fly a plane like Miss Ramola's brother.'

'And what about you, Prakash?' asked Bina.

Prakash just smiled and said, 'Maybe I'll be a flute-player,' and he put the flute to he lips and played a sweet melody.

'Well, the world needs flute-players too,' said Bina, as they fell into step beside him.

The leopard had been stalking a barking deer. She paused when she heard the flute and the voices of the children. Her own young ones were growing quickly, but the girl and the two boys did not look much older.

They had started singing their favourite song again.

Five more miles to go!
We climb through rain and snow,
A river to cross...
A mountain to pass...
Now we've four more miles to go!

The leopard waited until they had passed, before returning to the trail of the barking deer.

UNCLE KEN'S RUMBLE IN THE JUNGLE

Uncle Ken drove Grandfather's old Fiat along the Forest road at an incredible 30mph, scattering pheasants, partridges and junglefowl as he scattered along. He had come in search of the disappearing red junglefowl, and I could see why the bird had disappeared. Too many noisy human beings had invaded its habitat.

By the time we reached the forest rest house, one of the car doors had fallen off its hinges, and a large lantana bush had got entwined in the bumper.

'Never mind,' said Uncle Ken. 'It's all part of the adventure.'

The rest house had been reserved for Uncle Ken, thanks to Grandfather's good relations with the forest department. But I was the only other person in the car. No one else would trust himself or herself to Uncle Ken's driving. He treated a car as though it were a low-flying aircraft having some difficulty in getting off the runway.

As we arrived at the rest house, a number of hens made a dash for safety.

'Look, junglefowl!' exclaimed Uncle Ken.

'Domestic fowl,' I said, 'They must belong to the forest guards.'

I was right, of course. One of the hens was destined to be served up as chicken curry later that day. The jungle birds avoided the neighbourhood of the rest house, just in case they were mistaken for poultry and went into the cooking-pot.

Uncle Ken was all for starting his search right away, and after a brief interval during which we were served with tea and pakoras (prepared by the forest guard, who it turned out was also a good cook), we set off on foot into the jungle in search of the elusive red junglefowl.

'No tigers around here! Are there?' asked Uncle Ken, just to be on the safe side.

'No tigers on this range,' said the guard, 'Just elephants.'

Uncle Ken wasn't afraid of elephants. He'd been for numerous elephants rides at the Lucknow zoo. He'd also seen Sabu in *Elephant Boy*.

A small wooden bridge took us across a little river, and then we were in third jungle, following the forest guard who led us along a path that was frequently blocked by broken tree branches and pieces of bamboo.

'Why all these broken branches?' asked Uncle Ken.

'The elephants, sir,' replied our guard, 'They passed through last night. They like certain leaves, as well as young bamboo shoots.'

We saw a number of spotted deer and several pheasants, but no red junglefowl.

That evening we sat out on the verandahh of the rest house. All was silent except for the distant trumpeting of elephants. Then, from the stream, came the chanting of hundreds of frogs.

There were tenors and baritones, sopranos and contraltos, and occasionally a bass deep enough to have pleased the great Chaliapin. They sang duets and quartets from *La Boheme* and other Italian operas, drowning out all other jungle sounds except for the occasional cry of a jackal doing his best to join in.

'We might as well sing too,' said Uncle Ken, and began singing the 'Indian Love Call' in his best Nelson Eddy manner.

The frogs fell silent, obviously awestruck; but instead of receiving an answering love-call, Uncle Ken was answered by even more strident jackal calls—not one, but several—with the result that all self-respecting denizens of the forest fled from the vicinity, and we saw no wildlife that night apart from a frightened rabbit that sped across the clearing and vanished into the darkness.

Early next morning we renewed our efforts to track down the Red junglefowl, but it remained elusive. Returning to the rest house dusty and weary, Uncle Ken exclaimed: 'There it is—a Red junglefowl!'

But it turned out to be the caretaker's cock-bird, a handsome fellow all red and gold, but not the jungle variety.

Disappointed, Uncle Ken decided to return to civilization. Another night in the rest house did not appeal to him. He had run out of songs to sing.

In any case, the weather had changed overnight and a light drizzle was falling as we started out. This had turned to a steady downpour by the time we reached the bridge across the Suseva River. And standing in the middle of the bridge was an elephant.

He was a long tusker and he didn't look too friendly.

Uncle Ken blew his horn, and that was a mistake.

It was a strident, penetrating horn, highly effective on city roads but out of place in the forest.

The elephant took it as a challenge, and returned the blast of the horn with a shrill trumpeting of its own. It took a few steps forward. Uncle Ken put the car into reverse.

'Is there another way out of here?' he asked.

'There's a side road,' I said, recalling an earlier trip with Grandfather, 'It will take us to the Kansrao railway station.'

'What ho!' cried Uncle Ken. 'To the station we go!'

And he turned the car and drove back until we came to the turning.

The narrow road was now a rushing torrent of rain water and all Uncle Ken's driving-skills were put to the test. He had on one occasion driven through a brick wall, so he knew all about obstacles; but they were usually stationary ones.

'More elephants,' I said, as two large pachyderms loomed out of the rain-drenched forest.

'Elephants to the right of us, elephants to the left of us!' chanted Uncle Ken, misquoting Tennyson's 'The Charge of the Light Brigade', 'Into the valley of death rode the six hundred!'

'There are now three of them,' I observed.

'Not my lucky number,' said Uncle Ken and pressed hard on the accelerator. We lurched forward, almost running over a terrified barking-deer.

'Is four your lucky number, Uncle Ken?'

'Why do you ask?'

'Well, there are now four of them behind us. And they are catching up quite fast!'

'I see the station ahead,' cried Uncle Ken, as we drove into a clearing where a tiny railway station stood like a beacon of safety in the wilderness.

The car came to a grinding halt. We abandoned it and ran for the building.

The station-master saw our predicament, and beckoned to us to enter the station building, which was little more than a two-room shed and platform. He took us inside his tiny control room and shut the steel gate behind us.

'The elephants won't bother you here,' he said. 'But say goodbye to your car.'

We looked out of the window and were horrified to see Grandfather's Fiat overturned by one of the elephants, while another proceeded to trample it underfoot. The other elephants joined in the mayhem and soon the car was a flattened piece of junk.

'I'm station-master Abdul Rauf,' the station-master introduced himself. 'I know a good scrap dealer in Doiwala. I'll give you his address.'

'But how do we get out of here?' asked Uncle Ken.

'Well, it's only an hour's walk to Doiwala, not with those elephants around. Stay and have a cup of tea. The Dehra Express will pass through shortly. It stops for a few minutes. And it's only half-an-hour to Dehra from here.' He punched out a couple of rail tickets, 'Here you are, my friends. Just two rupees each. The cheapest rail journey in India. And these tickets carry an insurance value of two lakh rupees each, should an accident befall you between here and Dehradun.'

Uncle Ken's eyes lit up.

'You mean, if one of us falls out of the train?' he asked.

'Out of the moving train,' clarified the station-master. 'There will be an enquiry, of course, some people try to fake an accident.'

But Uncle Ken decided against falling out of the train and making a fortune. He'd had enough excitement for the day. We got home safely enough, taking a pony-cart from Dehradun station to our house.

'Where's my car?' asked Grandfather, as we staggered up the verandahh steps.

'It had a small accident,' said Uncle Ken. 'We left it outside the Kansrao railway station. I'll collect it later.'

'I'm starving,' I said. 'Haven't eaten since morning.'

'Well, come and have your dinner,' said Granny. 'I've made something special for you. One of your grandfather's hunting friends sent us a junglefowl. I've made a nice roast. Try it with apple sauce.'

Uncle Ken did not ask if the junglefowl was red, grey, or technicoloured. He was first to the dining table.

Granny had anticipated this, and served me with a chicken leg, giving the other leg to grandfather.

'I rather fancy the breast myself,' she said, and this left Uncle Ken with a long and scrawny neck—which was more than he deserved.

THE STREET OF LOST HOMES

'What did you want to go there for?' asked Hassan, when I knocked on his door at the crack of dawn.

'It was raining heavily, and I stopped near the gate to take shelter. A boy invited me in, his mother gave me something to eat, and I ended up spending the night in the raja's bedroom.' I said nothing about screams in the night or the skeleton in the bed.

Hassan presented me with a bun and a glass of hot sweet tea.

'Nobody goes there,' he said. 'The place has a bad name.'

'And why's that?'

'The old raja was a bad man. Tortured his wives, or so it was said.'

'And what happened to him?'

'Got killed in a hunting accident, in the jungles next to Bijnor. He went after a tiger, but the tiger got to him first. Bit his head off! Everyone was pleased. His younger brother inherited the palace, but he never comes here. I think he still lives somewhere near the Nepal border.'

'And the people who still live in the palace?'

'Poor relations, I think. Offspring from one of the raja's

wives or concubines—no one quite knows, or even cares. We don't see much of them, and they keep to themselves. But people avoid the place, they say it is still full of evil, haunted by the old scoundrel whose cruelty has left its mark on the walls... It should be pulled down!'

'It's falling down of its own accord,' I said. 'Most of it is already a ruin.'

◆

Later that morning I found Hassan closing the doors of the bakery.

'Are you off somewhere?' I asked.

He nodded. 'Down to Rajpur. My boys are at school and my daughter is too young to look after the place.'

'It's urgent, then?'

'That fool of a youth, Sunil, has got into trouble. Picking someone's pocket, no doubt. They are holding him at the Rajpur thana.

'But why do you have to go? Doesn't he have any relatives?'

'None of any use. His father died some time back. He did me a favour once. More than a favour—he saved my life. So I must help the boy, even if he is a badmash.'

'I'll come with you,' I said on an impulse. 'Is it very far?'

'Rajpur is at the bottom of the hill. About an hour's walk down the footpath. Quicker than walking up to Mussoorie and waiting for a bus.'

I joined him on the road, and together we set off down the old path.

We passed Fairy Glen—the ruin where I had passed the night. It looked quite peaceful in the April sunshine. The gate was closed. There was no sign of the boy or his mother, my hosts of the previous night. It would have been embarrassing to meet them, for I had left in an almighty hurry. There was no sign of the big black bird, either. Only a couple of mynas squabbling on the wall, and a black-faced langur swinging from the branch of an oak.

I had some difficulty in keeping up with Hassan. Although he was over forty and had the beginnings of a paunch, he was a sturdy fellow, and he had the confident, even stride of someone who had spent most of his life in the hills.

The path was a steep one, and it began to level out only when it entered the foothills hamlet of Rajpur. At that time Rajpur was something of a ghost town. Some sixteen years earlier, most of its inhabitants, Muslims like Hassan, had fled or been killed by mobs during the communal strife that followed the partition of the country.

Rajpur had yet to recover. We passed empty, gutted buildings, some roofless, some without doors and windows. Weeds and small bushes grew out of the floors of abandoned houses. Successive monsoons had removed the mud or cement plaster from the walls, leaving behind bare brickwork which was beginning to crumble. The entire length of the street, where once there had been a hundred homes pulsating with life and human endeavour, now stood empty, homes only to jackals, snakes, and huge rock lizards.

Hassan stopped before an empty doorway. Behind it an empty courtyard. Behind it a wall with empty windows.

'I lived here once,' he said. 'My parents, younger brother, sister, my first wife...all of us worked together, making bread and buns and pastries for the rich folk in the houses along the

Dehra road. And in one night I lost everyone, everything—parents, brother, sister, wife... The fire swept through the mohalla, and those who ran out of their houses were cut down by swords and kirpans.'

I stopped and put a hand on his shoulder.

'It's hard for me to talk about it. Later, perhaps...' And he moved on.

The street of lost homes gave way to a small bazaar, the only visible sign of some sort of recovery. A young man from a nearby village ran the small dhaba where we stopped for tea and pakoras. He was too young to have any memories of 1947. And in India, town and countryside often appear to have completely different histories.

Hassan asked me to wait at the dhaba while he walked down to the local thana to enquire after Sunil.

'A thana is no place for a respectable person like you,' he said.

'In Delhi, the prisons are full of respectable people,' I said.

'But not respected anymore?'

'Well, some of them don't seem to be too bothered. They get bail, come out with a swagger, and drive home in their cars.'

'And what are their crimes?'

'The same as Sunil's. They pick pockets, but in a big way. You don't see them doing it. But carry on, I'll wait here for you.'

The dhak, or flame of the forest, was in flower, and I sat on a bench taking in the sights and sounds of summer's arrival in the valley. Scarlet bougainvillea cascaded over a low wall, and a flock of parrots flung themselves from one tall mango tree to another, sampling the young unripe fruit.

'Will there be a good crop this year?' I asked the young dhabawala.

'Should be, if the parrots and monkeys leave any for us.'

'You need a chowkidar,' I said, and thought of recommending Sunil. But Hassan came back without him.

'No magistrate in court today. We'll try again tomorrow. In the meantime, he gets board and lodging at government expense. He doesn't have to pick any pockets.'

'He will, if he gets a chance. It's an incurable disease.'

THE TUNNEL

It was almost noon, and the jungle was very still, very silent. Heat waves shimmered along the railway embankment where it cut a path through the tall evergreen trees. The railway lines were two straight black serpents disappearing into the tunnel in the hillside.

Suraj stood near the cutting, waiting for the mid-day train. It wasn't a station, and he wasn't catching a train. He was waiting so that he could watch the steam engine come roaring out of the tunnel.

He had cycled out of the town and taken the jungle path until he had come to a small village. He had left the cycle there, and walked over a low, scrub-covered hill and down to the tunnel exit.

Now he looked up. He had heard, in the distance, the shrill whistle of the engine. He couldn't see anything, because the train was approaching from the other side of the hill; but presently a sound, like distant thunder, issued from the tunnel, and he knew the train was coming through.

A second or two later, the steam engine shot out of the tunnel, snorting and puffing like some green, black and gold dragon, some beautiful monster out of Suraj's dreams. Showering sparks left and right, it roared a challenge to the jungle.

Instinctively, Suraj stepped back a few paces. And then the train had gone, leaving only a plume of smoke to drift lazily over tall shisham trees.

The jungle was still again. No one moved. Suraj turned from his contemplation of the drifting smoke and began walking along the embankment towards the tunnel.

The tunnel grew darker as he walked further into it. When he had gone about twenty yards, it became pitch black. Suraj had to turn and look back at the opening to reassure himself that there was still daylight outside. Ahead of him, the tunnel's other opening was just a small round circle of light.

The tunnel was still full of smoke from the train, but it would be several hours before another train came through. Till then, it belonged to the jungle again.

Suraj didn't stop, because there was nothing to do in the tunnel and nothing to see. He had simply wanted to walk through, so that he would know what the inside of a tunnel was really like. The walls were damp and sticky. A bat flew past. A lizard scuttled between the lines.

Coming straight from the darkness into the light, Suraj was dazzled by the sudden glare. He put a hand up to shade his eyes and looked up at the tree-covered hillside. He thought he saw something moving between the trees.

It was just a flash of orange and gold, and a long swishing tail. It was there between the trees for a second or two, and then it was gone.

About fifty feet from the entrance to the tunnel stood the watchman's hut. Marigolds grew in front of the hut, and at the back there was a small vegetable patch. It was the watchman's duty to inspect the tunnel and keep it clear of obstacles. Every day, before the train came through, he would walk the length of the tunnel. If all was well, he would return to his hut and take a nap. If something was wrong, he would walk back up the line and wave a red flag and the engine-driver would slow down. At night, the watchman lit an oil lamp and made a similar inspection of the tunnel. Of course, he could not stop the train if there was a porcupine on the line. But if there was any danger to the train, he'd go back up the line and wave his lamp to the approaching engine. If all was well, he'd hang his lamp at the door of the hut and go to sleep.

He was just settling down on his cot for an afternoon nap when he saw the boy emerge from the tunnel. He waited until Suraj was only a few feet away and then said: 'Welcome, welcome, I don't often have visitors. Sit down for a while, and tell me why you were inspecting my tunnel.'

'Is it your tunnel?' asked Suraj.

'It is,' said the watchman. 'It is truly my tunnel, since no one else will have anything to do with it. I have only lent it to the government.'

Suraj sat down on the edge of the cot.

'I wanted to see the train come through,' he said. 'And then, when it had gone, I thought I'd walk through the tunnel.'

'And what did you find in it?'

'Nothing. It was very dark. But when I came out, I thought I saw an animal—up on the hill—but I'm not sure, it moved away very quickly.'

'It was a leopard you saw,' said the watchman. 'My leopard.'

'Do you own a leopard too?'

'I do.'

'And do you lend it to the government?'

'I do not.'

'Is it dangerous?'

'No, it's a leopard that minds its own business. It comes to this range for a few days every month.'

'Have you been here a long time?' asked Suraj.

'Many years. My name is Sunder Singh.'

'My name's Suraj.'

'There's one train during the day. And another during the night. Have you seen the night mail come through the tunnel?'

'No. At what time does it come?'

'About nine o'clock, if it isn't late. You could come and sit here with me, if you like. And after it has gone, I'll take you home.'

'I shall ask my parents,' said Suraj. 'Will it be safe?'

'Of course. It's safer in the jungle than in the town. Nothing happens to me out here, but last month when I went into the town, I was almost run over by a bus.'

Sunder Singh yawned and stretched himself out on the cot. 'And now I'm going to take a nap, my friend. It is too hot to be up and about in the afternoon.'

'Everyone goes to sleep in the afternoon,' complained Suraj. 'My father lies down as soon as he's had his lunch.'

'Well, the animals also rest in the heat of the day. It is only the tribe of boys who cannot, or will not, rest.'

Sunder Singh placed a large banana-leaf over his face to keep away the flies, and was soon snoring gently. Suraj stood up, looking up and down the railway tracks. Then he began walking back to the village.

The following evening, towards dusk, as the flying foxes swooped silently out of the trees, Suraj made his way to the watchman's hut.

It had been a long hot day, but now the earth was cooling, and a light breeze was moving through the trees. It carried with it a scent of mango blossoms, the promise of rain.

Sunder Singh was waiting for Suraj. He had watered his small garden, and the flowers looked cool and fresh. A kettle was boiling on a small oil stove.

'I'm making tea,' he said. 'There's nothing like a glass of hot tea while waiting for a train.'

They drank their tea, listening to the sharp notes of the tailorbird and the noisy chatter of the seven-sisters. As the brief twilight faded, most of the birds fell silent. Sunder Singh lit his oil-lamp and said it was time for him to inspect the tunnel. He moved off towards the tunnel, while Suraj sat on the cot, sipping his tea. In the dark, the trees seemed to move closer to him. And the night life of the forest was conveyed on the breeze—the sharp call of a barking deer, the cry of a fox, the quaint *tonk-tonk* of a nightjar. There were some sounds that Suraj couldn't recognize—sounds that came from the trees, creakings and whisperings, as though the trees were coming alive, stretching their limbs in the dark, shifting a little, reflexing their fingers.

Sunder Singh stood inside the tunnel, trimming his lamp. The night sounds were familiar to him and he did not give them much thought; but something else—a padded footfall, a rustle of dry leaves—made him stand alert for a few seconds, peering into the darkness. Then, humming softly to himself, he returned to where Suraj was waiting. Another ten minutes remained for the night mail to arrive.

As Sunder Singh sat down on the cot beside Suraj, a new sound reached both of them quite distinctly—a rhythmic sawing sound, as if someone was cutting through the branch of a tree.

'What's that?' whispered Suraj.

'It's the leopard,' said Sunder Singh.

'I think it's in the tunnel.'

'The train will soon be here,' reminded Suraj.

'Yes, my friend. And if we don't drive the leopard out of the tunnel, it will be run over and killed. I can't let that happen.'

'But won't it attack us if we try to drive it out?' asked Suraj, beginning to share the watchman's concern.

'Not this leopard. It knows me well. We have seen each other many times. It has a weakness for goats and stray dogs, but it won't harm us. Even so, I'll take my axe with me. You stay here, Suraj.'

'No, I'm going with you. It'll be better than sitting here alone in the dark!'

'All right, but stay close behind me. And remember, there's nothing to fear.'

Raising his lamp high, Sunder Singh advanced into the tunnel, shouting at the top of his voice to try and scare away the animal. Suraj followed close behind, but he found he was unable to do any shouting. His throat was quite dry.

They had gone just about twenty paces into the tunnel when the light from the lamp fell upon the leopard. It was crouching between the tracks, only fifteen feet away from them. It was not a very big leopard, but it looked lithe and sinewy. Baring its teeth and snarling, it went down on its belly, tail twitching.

Suraj and Sunder Singh both shouted together. Their voices

rang through the tunnel. And the leopard, uncertain as to how many terrifying humans were there in the tunnel with him, turned swiftly and disappeared into the darkness.

To make sure that it had gone, Sunder Singh and Suraj walked the length of the tunnel. When they returned to the entrance, the rails were beginning to hum. They knew the train was coming.

Suraj put his hand to the rails and felt its tremor. He heard the distant rumble of the train. And then the engine came round the bend, hissing at them, scattering sparks into the darkness, defying the jungle as it roared through the steep sides of the cutting. It charged straight at the tunnel, and into it, thundering past Suraj like the beautiful dragon of his dreams.

And when it had gone, the silence returned and the forest seemed to breathe, to live again. Only the rails still trembled with the passing of the train.

And they trembled to the passing of the same train, almost a week later, when Suraj and his father were both travelling in it.

Suraj's father was scribbling in a notebook, doing his accounts. Suraj sat at an open window staring out at the darkness. His father was going to Delhi on a business trip and had decided to take the boy along. ('I don't know where he gets to, most of the time,' he'd complained. 'I think it's time he learnt something about my business.')

The night mail rushed through the forest with its hundreds of passengers. Tiny flickering lights came and went, as they passed small villages on the fringe of the jungle.

Suraj heard the rumble as the train passed over a small bridge. It was too dark to see the hut near the cutting, but he knew they must be approaching the tunnel. He strained his eyes looking out into the night; and then, just as the engine let out a shrill whistle, Suraj saw the lamp.

He couldn't see Sunder Singh, but he saw the lamp, and he knew that his friend was out there.

The train went into the tunnel and out again; it left the jungle behind and thundered across the endless plains; and Suraj stared out at the darkness, thinking of the lonely cutting in the forest, and the watchman with the lamp who would always remain a firefly for those travelling thousands, as he lit up the darkness for steam engines and leopards.

A SPECIAL TREE

One day, when Rakesh was six, he walked home from the Mussoorie bazaar eating cherries. They were a little sweet, a little sour; small, bright red cherries, which had come all the way from the Kashmir Valley.

Here in the Himalayan foothills where Rakesh lived, there were not many fruit trees. The soil was stony, and the dry cold winds stunted the growth of most plants. But on the more sheltered slopes there were forests of oak and deodar.

Rakesh lived with his grandfather on the outskirts of Mussoorie, just where the forest began. His father and mother lived in a small village fifty miles away, where they grew maize and rice and barley in narrow terraced fields on the lower slopes of the mountain. But there were no schools in the village, and Rakesh's parents were keen that he should go to school. As soon as he was of school-going age, they sent him to stay with his grandfather in Mussoorie.

Grandfather had a little cottage outside the town.

Rakesh was on his way home from school when he bought the cherries. He paid fifty paise for the bunch. It took him about half-an-hour to walk home, and by the time he reached the cottage there were only three cherries left.

'Have a cherry, Grandfather,' he said, as soon as he saw his grandfather in the garden.

Grandfather took one cherry and Rakesh promptly ate the other two. He kept the last seed in his mouth for some time, rolling it round and round on his tongue until all the tang had gone. Then he placed the seed on the palm of his hand and studied it.

'Are cherry seeds lucky?' asked Rakesh.

'Of course.'

'Then I'll keep it.'

'Nothing is lucky if you put it away. If you want luck, you must put it to some use.'

'What can I do with a seed?'

'Plant it.'

So Rakesh found a small space and began to dig up a flowerbed.

'Hey, not there,' said Grandfather, 'I've sown mustard in that bed. Plant it in that shady corner, where it won't be disturbed.'

Rakesh went to a corner of the garden where the earth was soft and yielding. He did not have to dig. He pressed the seed into the soil with his thumb and it went right in.

Then he had his lunch, and ran off to play cricket with his friends, and forgot all about the cherry seed.

When it was winter in the hills, a cold wind blew down from the snows and went *whoo-whoo-whoo* in the deodar trees, and the garden was dry and bare. In the evenings Grandfather and Rakesh sat around a charcoal fire, and Grandfather told Rakesh stories—stories about people who turned into animals, and ghosts who lived in trees, and beans that jumped and stones that wept—and in turn Rakesh would read to him from the newspaper, Grandfather's eyesight being rather weak. Rakesh found the newspaper very dull—especially after the stories—but Grandfather wanted all the news...

They knew it was spring when the wild duck flew north again, to Siberia. Early in the morning, when he got up to chop wood and light a fire, Rakesh saw the V-shaped formation streaming northward, the calls of the birds carrying clearly through the thin mountain air.

One morning in the garden he bent to pick up what he thought was a small twig and found to his surprise that it was well-rooted. He stared at it for a moment, then ran to fetch Grandfather, calling, 'Dada, come and look, the cherry tree has come up!'

'What cherry tree?' asked Grandfather, who had forgotten about it.

'The seed we planted last year—look, it's come up!'

Rakesh went down on his haunches, while Grandfather bent almost double and peered down at the tiny tree. It was about four inches high.

'Yes, it's a cherry tree,' said Grandfather. 'You should water it now and then.'

Rakesh ran indoors and came back with a bucket of water.

'Don't drown it!' said Grandfather.

Rakesh gave it a sprinkling and circled it with pebbles.

'What are the pebbles for?' asked Grandfather.

'For privacy,' said Rakesh.

He looked at the tree every morning but it did not seem to be growing very fast, so he stopped looking at it except quickly, out of the corner of his eye. And, after a week or two, when he allowed himself to look at it properly, he found that it had grown—at least an inch!

That year the monsoon rains came early and Rakesh plodded to and from school in raincoat and chappals. Ferns sprang from the trunks of trees, strange-looking lilies came up in the long grass, and even when it wasn't raining the trees dripped and mist came curling up the valley. The cherry tree grew quickly in this season.

It was about two-feet high when a goat entered the garden and ate all the leaves. Only the main stem and two thin branches remained.

'Never mind,' said Grandfather, seeing that Rakesh was upset. 'It will grow again, cherry trees are tough.'

Towards the end of the rainy season new leaves appeared on the tree. Then a woman cutting grass scrambled down the hillside, her scythe swishing through the heavy monsoon foliage. She did not try to avoid the tree: one sweep, and the cherry tree was cut in two.

When Grandfather saw what had happened, he went after the woman and scolded her; but the damage could not be repaired.

'Maybe it will die now,' said Rakesh.

'Maybe,' said Grandfather.

But the cherry tree had no intention of dying.

By the time summer came round again, it had sent out several new shoots with tender green leaves. Rakesh had grown taller too. He was eight now, a sturdy boy with curly black hair and deep black eyes. 'Blackberry eyes,' Grandfather called them.

That monsoon Rakesh went home to his village, to help his father and mother with the planting and ploughing and sowing. He was thinner but stronger when he came back to Grandfather's house at the end of the rains to find that the cherry tree had grown another foot. It was now up to his chest.

Even when there was rain, Rakesh would sometimes water the tree. He wanted it to know that he was there.

One day he found a bright green praying-mantis perched on a branch, peering at him with bulging eyes. Rakesh let it remain there; it was the cherry tree's first visitor.

The next visitor was a hairy caterpillar, who started making a meal of the leaves. Rakesh removed it quickly and dropped it on a heap of dry leaves.

'Come back when you're a butterfly,' he said.

Winter came early. The cherry tree bent low with the weight of snow. Field mice sought shelter in the roof of the cottage. The road from the valley was blocked, and for several days there was no newspaper, and this made Grandfather quite grumpy. His stories began to have unhappy endings.

In February it was Rakesh's birthday. He was nine—and the tree was four, but almost as tall as Rakesh.

One morning, when the sun came out, Grandfather came into the garden to 'let some warmth get into my bones,' as he put it. He stopped in front of the cherry tree, stared at it for a few moments, and then called out, 'Rakesh! Come and look! Come quickly before it falls!'

Rakesh and Grandfather gazed at the tree as though it had performed a miracle. There was a pale pink blossom at the end of a branch.

The following year there were more blossoms. And suddenly the tree was taller than Rakesh, even though it was less than half his age. And then it was taller than Grandfather, who was older than some of the oak trees.

But Rakesh had grown too. He could run and jump and climb trees as well as most boys, and he read a lot of books, although he still liked listening to Grandfather's tales.

In the cherry tree, bees came to feed on the nectar in the blossoms, and tiny birds pecked at the blossoms and broke them off. But the tree kept blossoming right through the spring, and there were always more blossoms than birds.

That summer there were small cherries on the tree. Rakesh tasted one and spat it out.

'It's too sour,' he said.

'They'll be better next year,' said Grandfather.

But the birds liked them—especially the bigger birds, such as the bulbuls and scarlet minivets—and they flitted in and out of the foliage, feasting on the cherries.

On a warm sunny afternoon, when even the bees looked sleepy, Rakesh was looking for Grandfather without finding him in any of his favourite places around the house. Then he looked out of the bedroom window and saw Grandfather reclining on a cane chair under the cherry tree.

'There's just the right amount of shade here,' said Grandfather. 'And I like looking at the leaves.'

'They're pretty leaves,' said Rakesh. 'And they are always ready to dance, if there's a breeze.'

After Grandfather had come indoors, Rakesh went into the garden and lay down on the grass beneath the tree. He gazed up through the leaves at the great blue sky; and turning on his side, he could see the mountains striding away into the clouds. He was still lying beneath the tree when the evening shadows crept across the garden. Grandfather came back and sat down beside Rakesh, and they waited in silence until the stars came out and the nightjar began to call. In the forest below, the crickets and cicadas began tuning up; and suddenly the trees were full of the sound of insects.

'There are so many trees in the forest,' said Rakesh. 'What's so special about this tree? Why do we like it so much?'

'We planted it ourselves,' said Grandfather. That's why it's special.'

'Just one small seed,' said Rakesh, and he touched the smooth bark of the tree that he had grown. He ran his hand along the trunk of the tree and put his finger to the tip of a leaf. 'I wonder,' he whispered. 'Is this what it feels to be God?'

GETTING GRANNY'S GLASSES

Granny could hear the distant roar of the river and smell the pine needles beneath her feet, and feel the presence of her grandson, Mani; but she couldn't see the river or the trees; and of her grandson she could only make out his fuzzy hair, and sometimes, when he was very close, his blackberry eyes and the gleam of his teeth when he smiled.

Granny wore a pair of old glasses; she'd been wearing them for well over ten years, but her eyes had grown steadily weaker, and the glasses had grown older and were now scratched and spotted, and there was very little she could see through them. Still, they were better than nothing. Without them, everything was just a topsy-turvy blur.

Of course, Granny knew her way about the house and the fields, and on a clear day she could see the mountains—the mighty Himalayan snow peaks—striding away into the sky; but it was felt by Mani and his father that it was high time Granny had her eyes tested and got herself new glasses.

'Well, you know we can't get them in the village,' said Granny.

Mani said, 'You'll have to go to the eye hospital in Mussoorie.

That's the nearest town.'

'But that's a two-day journey,' protested Granny. 'First I'd have to walk to Nain Market, twelve miles at least, spend the night there at your Uncle's place, and then catch a bus for the rest of the journey! You know how I hate buses. And it's ten years since I walked all the way to Mussoorie. That was when I had these glasses made.'

'Well, it's still there,' said Mani's father.

'What is still there?'

'Mussoorie.'

'And the eye hospital?'

'That too.'

'Well, my eyes are not too bad, really,' said Granny, looking for excuses. She did not feel like going far from the village; in particular, she did not want to be parted from Mani. He was eleven and quite capable of looking after himself, but Granny had brought him up ever since his mother had died when he was only a year old. She was his Nani (maternal grandmother), and had cared for boy and father, and cows and hens and household, all these years, with great energy and devotion.

'I can manage quite well,' she said. 'As long as I can see what's right in front of me, there's no problem. I know you got a ball in your hand, Mani; please don't bounce it off the cow.'

'It's not a ball, Granny; it's an apple.'

'Oh, is it?' said Granny, recovering quickly from her mistake. 'Never mind, just don't bounce it off the cow. And don't eat too many apples!'

'Now listen,' said Mani's father sternly, 'I know you don't want to go anywhere. But we're not sending you off on your own. I'll take you to Mussoorie.'

'And leave Mani here by himself? How could you even think of doing that?'

'Then I'll take you to Mussoorie,' said Mani eagerly. 'We can leave father on his own, can't we? I've been to Mussoorie before, with my school friends. I know where we can stay. But—' He paused a moment and looked doubtfully from his father to his grandmother. 'You wouldn't be able to walk all the way to Nain, would you, Granny?'

'Of course I can walk,' said Granny. 'I may be going blind, but there's nothing wrong with my legs!'

That was true enough. Only day before they'd found Granny in the walnut tree, tossing walnuts, not very accurately, into a large basket on the ground.

'But you're seventy, Granny.'

'What has that got to do with it? And besides, it's downhill to Nain.'

'And uphill coming back.'

'Uphill's easier!' said Granny.

Now that she knew Mani might be accompanying her, she was more than ready to make the journey.

The monsoon rains had begun, and in front of the small stone house a cluster of giant dahlias reared their heads. Mani had seen them growing in Nain and had brought some bulbs home. 'These are big flowers, Granny,' he'd said. 'You'll be able to see them better.'

She could indeed see the dahlias, splashes of red and yellow against the old stone of the cottage walls.

Looking at them now, Granny said, 'While we're in Mussoorie, we'll get some seeds and bulbs. And a new bell for the white cow. And a pullover for your father. And shoes for you.

Look, there's nothing much left of the ones you're wearing.'

'Now just a minute,' said Mani's father. 'Are you going there to get your eyes tested, or are you going on a shopping expedition? I've got only a hundred rupees to spare. You'll have to manage with that.'

'We'll manage,' said Mani. 'We'll sleep at the bus shelter.'

'No, we won't,' said Granny. 'I've got fifty rupees of my own. We'll stay at a hotel!'

Early next morning, in a light drizzle, Granny and Mani set out on the path to Nain.

Mani carried a small bedding-roll on his shoulder; Granny carried a large cloth shopping bag and an umbrella.

The path went through fields and around the brow of the hill and then began to wind here and there, up and down and around, as though it had a will of its own and no intention of going anywhere in particular. Travellers new to the area often left the path, because they were impatient or in a hurry, and thought there were quicker, better ways of reaching their destinations. Almost immediately they found themselves lost. For it was a wise path and a good path, and had found the right way of crossing the mountains after centuries of trial and error.

'Whenever you feel tired, we'll take rest,' said Mani.

'We've only just started out,' said Granny. 'We'll rest when you're hungry!'

They walked at a steady pace, without talking too much. A flock of parrots whirled overhead, flashes of red and green against the sombre sky. High in a spruce tree a barbet called monotonously. But there were no other sounds, except for the hiss and gentle patter of the rain.

Mani stopped to pick wild blackberries from a bush. Granny

wasn't fond of berries and didn't slacken her pace. Mani had to run to catch up with her. Soon his lips were purple with the juice from the berries.

The rain stopped and the sun came out. Below them, the light green of the fields stood out against the dark green of the forests, and the hills were bathed in golden sunshine.

Mani ran ahead.

'Can you see all right, Granny?' he called.

'I can see the path and I can see your white shirt. That's enough for now.'

'Well, watch out, there are some mules coming down the road.'

Granny stepped aside to allow the mules to pass. They clattered by, the mule-driver urging them on with a romantic song; but the last mule veered toward Granny and appeared to be heading straight for her. Granny saw it just in time. She knew that mules and ponies always preferred going around objects, if they could see what lay ahead of them, so she held out her open umbrella and the mule cantered round it without touching her.

Granny and Mani ate their light meal on the roadside, in the shade of a whispering pine, and drank from a spring a little further down the path.

By late afternoon they were directly above Nain.

'We're almost there,' said Mani. 'I can see the temple near Uncle's house.'

'I can't see a thing,' said Granny.

'That's because of the mist. There's a thick mist coming up the valley.'

It started raining heavily as they entered the small market

town on the banks of the river. Granny's umbrella was leaking badly. But they were soon drying themselves in Uncle's house, and drinking glasses of hot sweet milky tea.

Mani got up early the next morning and ran down the narrow street to bathe in the river. The swift but shallow mountain river was a tributary of the sacred Ganges, and its waters were held sacred too. As the sun rose, people thronged the steps leading down to the river, to bathe or pray or float flower offerings downstream.

As Mani dressed, he heard the blare of a bus horn. There was only one bus to Mussoorie. He scampered up the slope, wondering if they'd miss it. But Granny was waiting for him at the bus stop. She had already bought their tickets.

The motor road followed the course of the river, which thundered a hundred feet below. The bus was old and rickety, and rattled so much that the passengers could barely hear themselves speaking.

One of them was pointing to a spot below, where another bus had gone off the road a few weeks back, resulting in many casualties.

The driver appeared to be unaware of the accident. He drove at some speed, and whenever he went round a bend, everyone in the bus was thrown about. In spite of all the noise and confusion, Granny fell asleep; her head resting against Mani's shoulder.

Suddenly the bus came to a grinding halt. People were thrown forward in their seats. Granny's glasses fell off and had to be retrieved from the folds of someone else's umbrella.

'What's happening?' she asked. 'Have we arrived?'

'No, something is blocking the road,' said Mani.

'It's a landslide!' exclaimed someone, and all the passengers put their heads out of the windows to take a look.

It was a big landslide. Sometime in the night, during the heavy rain, earth and trees and bushes had given way and come crashing down, completely blocking the road. Nor was it over yet. Debris was still falling. Mani saw rocks hurtling down the hill and into the river.

'Not a suitable place for a bus stop,' observed Granny, who couldn't see a thing.

Even as she spoke, a shower of stones and small rocks came clattering down on the roof of the bus. Passengers cried out in alarm. The driver began reversing, as more rocks came crashing down.

'I never did trust motor roads,' said Granny.

The driver kept backing until they were well away from the landslide. Then everyone tumbled out of the bus. Granny and Mani were the last to get down.

They were told that it would take days to clear the road, and most of the passengers decided to return to Nain with the bus. But a few bold spirits agreed to walk to Mussoorie, taking a shortcut up the mountain which would by-pass the landslide.

'It's only ten miles from here by the footpath,' said one of them. 'A stiff climb, but we can make it by evening.'

Mani looked at Granny. 'Shall we go back?'

'What's ten miles?' said Granny. 'We did that yesterday.'

So they started climbing a narrow path, little more than a goat-track, which went steeply up the mountainside. But there was much huffing and puffing, and pausing for breath and by the time they got to the top of the mountain Granny and Mani were on their own. They could see a few stragglers far below;

the rest had retreated to Nain.

Granny and Mani stood on the summit of the mountain. They had it all to themselves. Their village was hidden by the range to the north. Far below rushed the river. Far above circled a golden eagle.

In the distance, on the next mountain, the houses of Mussoorie were white specks on the dark green hillside.

'Did you bring any food from Uncle's house?' asked Mani.

'Naturally,' said Granny. 'I knew you'd soon be hungry. There are pakoras and buns, and peaches from Uncle's garden.'

'Good!' said Mani, forgetting his tiredness. 'We'll eat as we go along. There's no need to stop.'

'Eating or walking?'

'Eating, of course. We'll stop when you're tired, Granny.'

'Oh, I can walk forever,' said Granny, laughing. 'I've been doing it all my life. And one day I'll just walk over the mountains and into the sky. But not if it's raining. This umbrella leaks badly.'

Down again they went, and up the next mountain, and over bare windswept hillsides, and up through a dark gloomy deodar forest. And then just as it was getting dark, they saw the lights of Mussoorie twinkling ahead of them.

As they came nearer, the lights increased, until presently they were in a brightly lit bazaar, swallowed up by crowds of shoppers, strollers, tourists and merrymakers. Mussoorie seemed a very jolly sort of place for those who had money to spend. Jostled in the crowd, Granny kept one hand firmly on Mani's shoulder so that she did not lose him.

They asked around for the cheapest hotel. But there were no cheap hotels. So they spent the night in a dharamsala adjoining the temple, where other pilgrims had taken shelter.

Next morning, at the eye hospital, they joined a long queue of patient patients. The eye specialist, a portly man in a suit and tie who himself wore glasses, dealt with the patients in a brisk but kind manner. After an hour's wait, Granny's turn came.

The doctor took one horrified look at Granny's glasses and dropped them in a wastebasket. Then he fished them out and placed them on his desk and said, 'On second thought, I think I'll send them to a museum. You should have changed your glasses years ago. They've probably done more harm than good.'

He examined Granny's eyes with a strong light, and said, 'Your eyes are very weak, but you're not going blind. We'll fit you up with a stronger pair of glasses.' Then he placed her in front of a board covered with letters in English and Hindi, large and small, and asked Granny if she could make them out.

'I can't even see the board,' said Granny.

'Well, can you see me?' asked the doctor.

'Some of you,' said Granny.

'I want you to see all of me,' said the doctor, and he balanced a wire frame on Granny's nose and began trying out different lenses.

Suddenly Granny could see much better. She saw the board and the biggest letters on it.

'Can you see me now?' asked the doctor.

'Most of you,' said Granny. And then added, by way of being helpful: 'There's quite a lot of you to see.'

'Thank you,' said the doctor. 'And now turn around and tell me if you can see your grandson.'

Granny turned, and saw Mani clearly for the first time in many years.

'Mani!' she exclaimed, clapping her hands with joy. 'How

nice you look! What a fine boy I've brought up! But you do need a haircut. And a wash. And buttons on your shirt. And a new pair of shoes. Come along to the bazaar!'

'First have your new glasses made,' said Mani, laughing. 'Then we'll go for shopping!'

A day later they were in a bus again, although no one knew how far it would be able to go. Sooner or later they would have to walk.

Granny had a window seat, and Mani sat beside her. He had new shoes and Granny had a new umbrella and they had also bought a thick woolen Tibetan pullover for Mani's father. And seeds and bulbs and a cowbell.

As the bus moved off, Granny looked eagerly out of the window. Each bend in the road opened up new vistas for her, and she could see many things that she hadn't seen for a long time—distant villages, people working in the fields, milkmen on the road, two dogs rushing along beside the bus, monkeys in the trees, and, most wonderful of all, a rainbow in the sky.

She couldn't see perfectly, of course, but she was very pleased with the improvement.

'What a large cow!' she remarked, pointing at a beast grazing on the hillside.

'It's not a cow, Granny,' said Mani. 'It's a buffalo.'

Granny was not to be discouraged. 'Anyway, I saw it,' she insisted.

While most of the people on the bus looked weary and bored, Granny continued to gaze out of the window, discovering new sights.

Mani watched for some time and listened to her excited chatter. Then his head began to nod. It dropped against Granny's shoulder, and remained there, comfortably supported. The bus swerved and jolted along the winding mountain road, but Mani was fast asleep.

TREMORS IN THE NIGHT

Not to be discouraged, we left the ghost town and continued our journey upriver, as far as the bus would take us. The road ended at Uttarkashi, for the simple reason that the bridge over the Bhagirathi had been washed away in a flash flood. The glaciers had been melting, and that, combined with torrential rain in the upper reaches, had brought torrents of muddy water rushing down the swollen river. Anything that came in its way vanished downstream.

We spent the night in a pilgrim shelter, built on a rocky ledge overlooking the river. All night we could hear the water roaring past below us. After a while, we became used to the unchanging sound; it became like a deep silence, and made our sleep deeper. Sometime before dawn, however, a sudden tremor had us trembling out of our cots.

'Earthquake!' shouted Sunil, making for the doorway and banging into the wall instead.

'Don't panic,' I said, feeling panicky.

'It will pass,' said Buddhoo.

The tremor did pass, but not before everyone in the shelter had rushed outside. There was the sound of rocks falling, and everyone rushed back again. 'Landslide!' someone shouted. Was it safer outside or inside? No one could be sure.

'It will pass,' said Buddhoo again, and went to sleep. Sunil began singing at the top of his voice: *'Pyar kiya to darna kya—* Why be afraid when we have loved.' I doubt Sunil had ever been in love, but it was a rousing song with which to meet death.

'Chup, beta!' admonished an old lady on her last pilgrimage to the abode of the gods. 'Say your prayers instead.'

The room fell silent. Outside, a dog started howling. Other dogs followed his example. No serenade this, but a mournful anticipation of things to come; for birds and beasts are more sensitive to the earth's tremors and inner convulsions than humans, who are no longer sensitive to nature's warnings.

A couple of jackals joined the chorus. Then a bird, probably a nightjar, set up a monotonous croak. I looked at my watch. It was 4 a.m, a little too early for birds to be greeting the break of day. But suddenly there was a twittering and cawing and chattering as all the birds in the vicinity passed on the message that something was amiss.

There was a rush of air and a window banged open.

The mountain shuddered. The building shook, rocked to and fro.

People began screaming and making for the door.

The door was flung open, but only a few escaped into the darkness.

Across the length of the room a chasm opened up. The lady saying her prayers fell into it. So did one or two others. Then the room and the people in it—those who were on the other side of the chasm—suddenly vanished.

There was the roar of falling masonry as half the building

slid down the side of the mountain.

We were left dangling in space.

'Let's get out of here quickly!' shouted Sunil.

We scrambled out of the door. In front of us, an empty void. I couldn't see a thing. Then Buddhoo took me by the hand and led me away from the crumbling building and on to the rocky ledge above the river.

The earth had stopped quaking, but the mountain had been shaken to its foundations, and rocks and trees were tumbling into the swollen river. The town was in darkness, the power station having shut down after the first tremor. Here and there a torch or lantern shone out of the darkness, and people could be heard wailing and shouting to each other as they roamed the streets in the rain. Somewhere a siren went off. It only seemed to add to the panic.

At 5 a.m, the rain stopped and the sky lightened. At six it was daybreak. A little later the sun came up. A beautiful morning, except for the devastation below.

THE ROOM OF MANY COLOURS

Last week I wrote a story, and all the time I was writing it I thought it was a good story; but when it was finished and I had read it through, I found that there was something missing, that it didn't ring true. So I tore it up. I wrote a poem, about an old man sleeping in the sun, and this was true, but it was finished quickly, and once again I was left with the problem of what to write next. And I remembered my father, who taught me to write; and I thought, why not write about my father, and about the trees we planted, and about the people I knew while growing up and about what happened on the way to growing up…

And so, like Alice, I must begin at the beginning, and in the beginning there was this red insect, just like a velvet button, which I found on the front lawn of the bungalow. The grass was still wet with overnight rain.

I placed the insect on the palm of my hand and took it into the house to show my father.

'Look, Dad,' I said, 'I haven't seen an insect like this before. Where has it come from?'

'Where did you find it?' he asked.

'On the grass.'

'It must have come down from the sky,' he said. 'It must have come down with the rain.'

Later he told me how the insect really happened but I preferred his first explanation. It was more fun to have it dropping from the sky.

I was seven at the time, and my father was thirty-seven, but, right from the beginning, he made me feel that I was old enough to talk to him about everything—insects, people, trees, steam engines, King George, comics, crocodiles, the Mahatma, the Viceroy, America, Mozambique and Timbuctoo. We took long walks together, explored old ruins, chased butterflies and waved to passing trains.

My mother had gone away when I was four, and I had very dim memories of her. Most other children had their mothers with them, and I found it a bit strange that mine couldn't stay. Whenever I asked my father why she'd gone, he'd say, 'You'll understand when you grow up.' And if I asked him *where* she had gone, he'd look troubled and say, 'I really don't know.' This was the only question of mine to which he didn't have an answer.

But I was quite happy living alone with my father; I had never known any other kind of life.

We were sitting on an old wall, looking out to sea at a couple of Arab dhows and a tram steamer, when my father said, 'Would you like to go to sea one day?'

'Where does the sea go?' I asked.

'It goes everywhere.'

'Does it go to the end of the world?'

'It goes right round the world. It's a round world.'

'It can't be.'

'It is. But it's so big, you can't see the roundness. When a fly sits on a watermelon, it can't see right round the melon, can it? The melon must seem quite flat to the fly. Well, in comparison to the world, we're much, much smaller than the tiniest of insects.'

'Have you been around the world?' I asked.

'No, only as far as England. That's where your grandfather was born.'

'And my grandmother?'

'She came to India from Norway when she was quite small. Norway is a cold land, with mountains and snow, and the sea cutting deep into the land. I was there as a boy. It's very beautiful, and the people are good and work hard.'

'I'd like to go there.'

'You will, one day. When you are older, I'll take you to Norway.'

'Is it better than England?'

'It's quite different.'

'Is it better than India?'

'It's quite different.'

'Is India like England?'

'No, it's different.'

'Well, what does "different" mean?'

'It means things are not the same. It means people are different. It means the weather is different. It means trees and birds and insects are different.'

'Are English crocodiles different from Indian crocodiles?'

'They don't have crocodiles in England.'

'Oh, then it must be different.'

'It would be a dull world if it was the same everywhere,' said my father.

He never lost patience with my endless questioning. If he wanted a rest, he would take out his pipe and spend a long time lighting it. If this took very long I'd find something else to do. But sometimes I'd wait patiently until the pipe was drawing, and then return to the attack.

'Will we always be in India?' I asked.

'No, we'll have to go away one day. You see, it's hard to explain, but it isn't really our country.'

'Ayah says it belongs to the King of England, and the jewels in his crown were taken from India, and that when the Indians get their jewels back the King will lose India! But first they have to get the crown from the King, but this is very difficult, she says, because the crown is always on his head. He even sleeps wearing his crown!'

Ayah was my nanny. She loved me deeply, and was always filling my head with strange and wonderful stories.

My father did not comment on Ayah's views. All he said was, 'We'll have to go away some day.'

'How long have we been here?' I asked.

'Two hundred years.'

'No, I mean us.'

'Well, you were born in India, so that's seven years for you.'

'Then can't I stay here?'

'Do you want to?'

'I want to go across the sea. But can we take Ayah with us?'

'I don't know, son. Let's walk along the beach.'

We lived in an old palace beside a lake. The palace looked like a ruin from the outside, but the rooms were cool and comfortable. We lived in one wing, and my father organized a small school in another wing. His pupils were the children of the Raja and the Raja's relatives. My father had started life in India as a tea planter, but he had been trained as a teacher and the idea of starting a school in a small state facing the Arabian Sea had appealed to him. The pay wasn't much, but we had a palace to live in, the latest 1938 model Hillman to drive about in, and a number of servants. In those days, of course, everyone had servants (although the servants did not have any!). Ayah was our own; but the cook, the bearer, the gardener, and the bhisti were all provided by the State.

Sometimes I sat in the schoolroom with the other children (who were all much bigger than me), sometimes I remained in the house with Ayah, sometimes I followed the gardener, Dukhi, about the spacious garden.

Dukhi means 'sad', and though I never could discover if the gardener had anything to feel sad about, the name certainly suited him. He had grown to resemble the drooping weeds that he was always digging up with a tiny spade. I seldom saw him standing up. He always sat on the ground with his knees well up to his chin, and attacked the weeds from this position. He could spend all day on his haunches, moving about the garden simply by shuffling his feet along the grass.

I tried to imitate his posture, sitting down on my heels and putting my knees into my armpits, but I could never hold the position for more than five minutes.

Time had no meaning in a large garden, and Dukhi never hurried. Life, for him, was not a matter of one year succeeding another, but of five seasons—winter, spring, hot weather, monsoon and autumn—arriving and departing. His seedbeds had always to be in readiness for the coming season, and he did not look any further than the next monsoon. It was impossible to tell his age. He may have been thirty-six or eighty-six. He was either very young for his years or very old for them.

Dukhi loved bright colours, especially reds and yellows. He liked strongly scented flowers, like jasmine and honeysuckle. He couldn't understand my father's preference for the more delicately perfumed petunias and sweetpeas. But I shared Dukhi's fondness for the common bright orange marigold, which is offered in temples and is used to make garlands and nosegays. When the garden was bare of all colour, the marigold would still be there, gay and flashy, challenging the sun.

Dukhi was very fond of making nosegays, and I liked to watch him at work. A sunflower formed the centrepiece. It was surrounded by roses, marigolds and oleander, fringed with green leaves, and bound together with silver thread. The perfume was overpowering. The nosegays were presented to me or my father on special occasions, that is, on a birthday or to guests of my father's who were considered important.

One day I found Dukhi making a nosegay, and said, 'No one is coming today, Dukhi. It isn't even a birthday.'

'It is a birthday, Chota Sahib,' he said. 'Little Sahib' was the title he had given me. It wasn't much of a title compared to Raja Sahib, Diwan Sahib or Burra Sahib, but it was nice to have a title at the age of seven.

'Oh,' I said. 'And is there a party, too?'

'No party.'

'What's the use of a birthday without a party? What's the use of a birthday without presents?'

'This person doesn't like presents—just flowers.'

'Who is it?' I asked, full of curiosity.

'If you want to find out, you can take these flowers to her.

She lives right at the top of that far side of the palace. There are twenty-two steps to climb. Remember that, Chota Sahib, you take twenty-three steps and you will go over the edge and into the lake!'

I started climbing the stairs.

It was a spiral staircase of wrought iron, and it went round and round and up and up, and it made me quite dizzy and tired.

At the top I found myself on a small balcony, which looked out over the lake and another palace, at the crowded city and the distant harbour. I heard a voice, a rather high, musical voice, saying (in English), 'Are you a ghost?' I turned to see who had spoken but found the balcony empty. The voice had come from a dark room.

I turned to the stairway, ready to flee, but the voice said, 'Oh, don't go, there's nothing to be frightened of!'

And so I stood still, peering cautiously into the darkness of the room.

'First, tell me—are you a ghost?'

'I'm a boy,' I said.

'And I'm a girl. We can be friends. I can't come out there, so you had better come in. Come along, I'm not a ghost either—not yet, anyway!'

As there was nothing very frightening about the voice, I stepped into the room. It was dark inside, and, coming in from the glare, it took me some time to make out the tiny, elderly lady seated on a cushioned gilt chair. She wore a red sari, lots of coloured bangles on her wrists, and golden earrings. Her hair was streaked with white, but her skin was still quite smooth and unlined, and she had large and very beautiful eyes.

'You must be Master Bond!' she said. 'Do you know who I am?'

'You're a lady with a birthday,' I said, 'but that's all I know. Dukhi didn't tell me any more.'

'If you promise to keep it a secret, I'll tell you who I am. You see, everyone thinks I'm mad. Do you think so too?'

'I don't know.'

'Well, you must tell me if you think so,' she said with a chuckle. Her laugh was the sort of sound made by the gecko, a little wall lizard, coming from deep down in the throat. 'I have a feeling you are a truthful boy. Do you find it very difficult to tell the truth?'

'Sometimes.'

'Sometimes. Of course, there are times when I tell lies—lots of little lies—because they're such fun! But would you call me a liar? I wouldn't, if I were you, but *would* you?'

'Are you a liar?'

'I'm asking you! If I were to tell you that I was a queen—that I *am* a queen—would you believe me?'

I thought deeply about this, and then said, 'I'll try to believe you.'

'Oh, but you *must* believe me. I'm a real queen, I'm a rani! Look, I've got diamonds to prove it!' And she held out her hands, and there was a ring on each finger, the stones glowing and glittering in the dim light. 'Diamonds, rubies, pearls and emeralds! Only a queen can have these!' She was most anxious that I should believe her.

'You must be a queen,' I said.

'Right!' she snapped. 'In that case, would you mind calling me "Your Highness"?'

'Your Highness,' I said.

She smiled. It was a slow, beautiful smile. Her whole face lit up.

'I could love you,' she said. 'But better still, I'll give you something to eat. Do you like chocolates?'

'Yes, Your Highness.'

'Well,' she said, taking a box from the table beside her, 'these have come all the way from England. Take two. Only two, mind, otherwise the box will finish before Thursday, and I don't want that to happen because I won't get any more till Saturday. That's when Captain MacWhirr's ship gets in, the *SS Lucy*, loaded with boxes and boxes of chocolates!'

'All for you?' I asked in considerable awe.

'Yes, of course. They have to last at least three months. I get them from England. I get only the best chocolates. I like them with pink, crunchy fillings, don't you?'

'Oh, yes!' I exclaimed, full of envy.

'Never mind,' she said, 'I may give you one, now and then— if you're very nice to me! Here you are, help yourself...' She pushed the chocolate box towards me.

I took a silver-wrapped chocolate, and then just as I was thinking of taking a second, she quickly took the box away.

'No more!' she said. 'They have to last till Saturday.'

'But I took only *one*,' I said with some indignation.

'Did you?' She gave me a sharp look, decided I was telling the truth, and said graciously, 'Well, in that case you can have another.'

Watching the Rani carefully, in case she snatched the box away again, I selected a second chocolate, this one with a green wrapper. I don't remember what kind of day it was outside, but I remember the bright green of the chocolate wrapper.

I thought it would be rude to eat the chocolates in front of a queen, so I put them in my pocket and said, 'I'd better go now. Ayah will be looking for me.'

'And when will you be coming to see me again?'

'I don't know,' I said.

'Your Highness.'

'Your Highness.'

'There's something I want you to do for me,' she said, placing one finger on my shoulder and giving me a conspiratorial look. 'Will you do it?'

'What is it, Your Highness?'

'What is it? Why do you ask? A real prince never asks where or why or whatever, he simply does what the princess asks of him. When I was a princess—before I became a queen, that is—I asked a prince to swim across the lake and fetch me a lily growing on the other bank.'

'And did he get it for you?'

'He drowned halfway across. Let that be a lesson to you. Never agree to do something without knowing what it is.'

'But I thought you said.'

'Never mind what I said. It's what I say that matters!'

'Oh, all right,' I said, fidgeting to be gone. 'What is it you want me to do?'

'Nothing.' Her tiny rosebud lips pouted and she stared sullenly at a picture on the wall. Now that my eyes had grown used to the dim light in the room, I noticed that the walls were hung with portraits of stout rajas and ranis, turbaned and bedecked in fine clothes. There were also portraits of Queen Victoria and King George V of England. And, in the centre of all this distinguished company, a large picture of Mickey Mouse.

'I'll do it if it isn't too dangerous,' I said.

'Then listen.' She took my hand and drew me towards her—what a tiny hand she had!—and whispered, 'I want a *red* rose from the palace garden. But be careful! Don't let Dukhi the gardener catch you. He'll know it's for me. He knows I love roses. And he hates me! I'll tell you why, one day. But if he catches you, he'll do something terrible.'

'To me?'

'No, to himself. That's much worse, isn't it? He'll tie himself into knots, or lie naked on a bed of thorns, or go on a long fast with nothing to eat but fruit, sweets and chicken! So you will be careful, won't you?'

'Oh, but he doesn't hate you,' I cried in protest, remembering the flowers he'd sent for her, and looking around I found that I'd been sitting on them. 'Look, he sent these flowers for your birthday!'

'Well, if he sent them for my birthday, you can take them back,' she snapped. 'But if he sent them for *me*...' and she suddenly softened and looked coy, 'then I might keep them. Thank you, my dear, it was a very sweet thought.' And she learnt forward as though to kiss me.

'It's late, I must go!' I said in alarm, and turning on my heels, ran out of the room and down the spiral staircase.

Father hadn't started lunch, or rather tiffin, as we called it then. He usually waited for me if I was late. I don't suppose he enjoyed eating alone.

For tiffin we usually had rice, a mutton curry (koftas or meat balls, with plenty of gravy, was my favourite curry), fried dal and a hot lime or mango pickle. For supper, we had English food—a soup, roast pork and fried potatoes, a rich gravy made by my father, and a custard or caramel pudding. My father enjoyed cooking, but it was only in the morning that he found time for it. Breakfast was his own creation. He cooked eggs in a variety of interesting ways, and favoured some Italian recipes which he had collected during a trip to Europe, long before I was born.

In deference to the feelings of our Hindu friends, we did not eat beef; but, apart from mutton and chicken, there was a plentiful supply of other meats—partridge, venison, lobster, and even porcupine!

'And where have you been?' asked my father, helping himself to rice as soon as he saw me come in.

'To the top of the old palace,' I said.

'Did you meet anyone there?'

'Yes, I met a tiny lady who told me she was a rani. She gave me chocolates.'

'As a rule, she doesn't like visitors.'

'Oh, she didn't mind me. But is she really a queen?'

'Well, she's the daughter of a maharaja. That makes her a princess. She never married. There's a story that she fell in love with a commoner, one of the palace servants, and wanted to marry him, but of course they wouldn't allow that. She became very melancholic, and started living all by herself in the old palace. They give her everything she needs, but she doesn't go out or have visitors. Everyone says she's mad.'

'How do they know?' I asked.

'Because she's different from other people, I suppose.'

'Is that being mad?'

'No. Not really, I suppose madness is not seeing things as others see them.'

'Is that very bad?'

'No,' said Father, who for once was finding it very difficult to explain something to me. 'But people who are like that—people whose minds are so different that they don't think, step by step, as we do, whose thoughts jump all over the place—such people are very difficult to live with...'

'Step by step,' I repeated. 'Step by step...'

'You aren't eating,' said my father. 'Hurry up, and you can come with me to school today.'

I always looked forward to attending my father's classes. He did not take me to the schoolroom very often, because he wanted school to be a treat, to begin with, and then, later, the routine wouldn't be so unwelcome.

Sitting there with older children, understanding only half of what they were learning, I felt important and part grown-up. And of course I did learn to read and write, although I first learnt to read upside-down, by means of standing in front of the others' desks and peering across at their books. Later, when I went to school, I had some difficulty in learning to read the right way up; and even today I sometimes read upside-down, for the sake of variety. I don't mean that I read standing on my head; simply that I held the book upside-down.

I had at my command a number of rhymes and jingles, the most interesting of these being 'Solomon Grundy'.

Solomon Grundy,
Born on a Monday,
Christened on Tuesday,
Married on Wednesday,
Took ill on Thursday,
Worse on Friday,

> Died on Saturday,
> Buried on Sunday:
> This is the end of
> Solomon Grundy.

Was that all that life amounted to, in the end? And were we all Solomon Grundys? These were questions that bothered me at the time. Another puzzling rhyme was the one that went:

> Hark, hark, the dogs do bark,
> The beggars are coming to town,
> Some in rags, some in bags,
> And some in velvet gowns.

This rhyme puzzled me for a long time. There were beggars aplenty in the bazaar, and sometimes they came to the house, and some of them did wear rags and bags (and some nothing at all) and the dogs did bark at them, but the beggar in the velvet gown never came our way.

'Who's this beggar in a velvet gown?' I asked my father.

'Not a beggar at all,' he said.

'Then why call him one?'

And I went to Ayah and asked her the same question, 'Who is the beggar in the velvet gown?'

'Jesus Christ,' said Ayah.

Ayah was a fervent Christian and made me say my prayers at night, even when I was very sleepy. She had, I think, Arab and Negro blood in addition to the blood of the Koli fishing community to which her mother had belonged. Her father, a sailor on an Arab dhow, had been a convert to Christianity. Ayah was a large, buxom woman, with heavy hands and feet and a slow, swaying gait that had all the grace and majesty of a royal elephant. Elephants for all their size are nimble creatures; and Ayah, too, was nimble, sensitive, and gentle with her big hands. Her face was always sweet and childlike.

Although a Christian, she clung to many of the beliefs of her parents, and loved to tell me stories about mischievous spirits and evil spirits, humans who changed into animals, and snakes who had been princes in their former lives.

There was the story of the snake who married a princess. At first the princess did not wish to marry the snake, whom she had met in a forest, but the snake insisted, saying, 'I'll kill you if you won't marry me,' and of course that settled the question. The snake led his bride away and took her to a great treasure. 'I was a prince in my former life,' he explained. 'This treasure is yours.' And then the snake very gallantly disappeared.

'Snakes,' declared Ayah, 'were very lucky omens if seen early in the morning.'

'But, what if the snake bites the lucky person?' I asked.

'He will be lucky all the same,' said Ayah with a logic that was all her own.

Snakes! There were a number of them living in the big garden, and my father had advised me to avoid the long grass. But I had seen snakes crossing the road (a lucky omen, according to Ayah) and they were never aggressive.

'A snake won't attack you,' said Father, 'provided you leave it alone. Of course, if you step on one it will probably bite.'

'Are all snakes poisonous?'

'Yes, but only a few are poisonous enough to kill a man. Others use their poison on rats and frogs. A good thing, too, otherwise during the rains the house would be taken over by the frogs.'

One afternoon, while Father was at school, Ayah found a snake in the bathtub. It wasn't early morning and so the snake couldn't have been a lucky one. Ayah was frightened and ran into the garden calling for help. Dukhi came running. Ayah ordered me to stay outside while they went after the snake.

And it was while I was alone in the garden—an unusual circumstance, since Dukhi was nearly always there—that I remembered the Rani's request. On an impulse, I went to the nearest rose bush and plucked the largest rose, pricking my thumb in the process.

And then, without waiting to see what had happened to the snake (it finally escaped), I started up the steps to the top of the old palace.

When I got to the top, I knocked on the door of the Rani's room. Getting no reply, I walked along the balcony until I reached another doorway. There were wooden panels around the door, with elephants, camels and turbaned warriors carved into it. As the door was open, I walked boldly into the room then stood still in astonishment. The room was filled with a strange light.

There were windows going right round the room, and each small windowpane was made of a different coloured glass. The sun that came through one window flung red and green and purple colours on the figure of the little Rani who stood there with her face pressed to the glass.

She spoke to me without turning from the window. 'This is my favourite room. I have all the colours here. I can see a different world through each pane of glass. Come, join me!' And she beckoned to me, her small hand fluttering like a delicate butterfly.

I went up to the Rani. She was only a little taller than me, and we were able to share the same windowpane.

'See, it's a red world!' she said.

The garden below, the palace and the lake, were all tinted red. I watched the Rani's world for a little while and then touched her on the arm and said, 'I have brought you a rose!'

She started away from me, and her eyes looked frightened. She would not look at the rose.

'Oh, why did you bring it?' she cried, wringing her hands.

'He'll be arrested now!'

'Who'll be arrested?'

'The prince, of course!'

'But *I* took it,' I said. 'No one saw me. Ayah and Dukhi were inside the house, catching a snake.'

'Did they catch it?' she asked, forgetting about the rose.

'I don't know. I didn't wait to see!'

'They should follow the snake, instead of catching it. It may lead them to a treasure. All snakes have treasures to guard.'

This seemed to confirm what Ayah had been telling me, and I resolved that I would follow the next snake that I met.

'Don't you like the rose, then?' I asked.

'Did you steal it?'

'Yes.'

'Good. Flowers should always be stolen. They're more fragrant then.'

Because of a man called Hitler war had been declared in Europe and Britain was fighting Germany.

In my comic papers, the Germans were usually shown as blundering idiots; so I didn't see how Britain could possibly lose the war, nor why it should concern India, nor why it should he necessary for my father to join up. But I remember his showing me a newspaper headline which said:

> BOMBS FALL ON BUCKINGHAM PALACE—KING AND QUEEN SAFE

I expect that had something to do with it.

He went to Delhi for an interview with the RAF and I was left in Ayah's charge.

It was a week I remember well, because it was the first time I had been left on my own. That first night I was afraid—afraid of the dark, afraid of the emptiness of the house, afraid of the howling of the jackals outside. The loud ticking of the clock was the only reassuring sound: clocks really made themselves heard in those days! I tried concentrating on the ticking, shutting out other sounds and the menace of the dark, but it wouldn't work. I thought I heard a faint hissing near the bed, and sat up, bathed in perspiration, certain that a snake was in the room. I shouted for Ayah and she came running, switching on all the lights.

'A snake!' I cried. 'There's a snake in the room!'

'Where, baba?'

'I don't know where, but I *heard* it.'

Ayah looked under the bed, and behind the chairs and tables, but there was no snake to be found. She persuaded me that I must have heard the breeze whispering in the mosquito curtains.

But I didn't want to be left alone.

'I'm coming to you,' I said and followed her into her small room near the kitchen.

Ayah slept on a low string cot. The mattress was thin, the blanket worn and patched up; but Ayah's warm and solid body made up for the discomfort of the bed. I snuggled up to her and was soon asleep.

I had almost forgotten the Rani in the old palace and was about to pay her a visit when, to my surprise, I found her in the garden. I had risen early that morning, and had gone running barefoot over the dew-drenched grass. No one was about, but I startled a flock of parrots and the birds rose screeching from a banyan tree and wheeled away to some other corner of the palace grounds. I was just in time to see a mongoose scurrying across the grass with an egg in its mouth. The mongoose must have been raiding the poultry farm at the palace.

I was trying to locate the mongoose's hideout, and was on all fours in a jungle of tall cosmos plants when I heard the rustle of clothes, and turned to find the Rani staring at me.

She didn't ask me what I was doing there, but simply said:

'I don't think he could have gone in there.'

'But I saw him go this way,' I said.

'Nonsense! He doesn't live in this part of the garden. He lives in the roots of the banyan tree.'

'But that's where the snake lives,' I said

'You mean the snake who was a prince. Well, that's whom I'm looking for!'

'A snake who was a prince!' I gaped at the Rani.

She made a gesture of impatience with her butterfly hands, and said, 'Tut, you're only a child, you can't understand. The prince lives in the roots of the banyan tree, but he comes out early every morning. Have you seen him?'

'No. But I saw a mongoose.'

The Rani became frightened. 'Oh dear, is there a mongoose in the garden? He might kill the prince!'

'How can a mongoose kill a prince?' I asked.

'You don't understand, Master Bond. Princes, when they

die, are born again as snakes.'

'*All* princes?'

'No, only those who die before they can marry.'

'Did your prince die before he could marry you?'

'Yes. And he returned to this garden in the form of a beautiful snake.'

'Well,' I said, 'I hope it wasn't the snake the water carrier killed last week.'

'He killed a snake!' The Rani looked horrified. She was quivering all over. 'It might have been the prince!'

'It was a brown snake,' I said.

'Oh, then it wasn't him.' She looked very relieved. 'Brown snakes are only ministers and people like that. It has to be a green snake to be a prince.'

'I haven't seen any green snakes here.'

'There's one living in the roots of the banyan tree. You won't kill it, will you?'

'Not if it's really a prince.'

'And you won't let others kill it?'

'I'll tell Ayah.'

'Good. You're on my side. But be careful of the gardener. Keep him away from the banyan tree. He's always killing snakes. I don't trust him at all.'

She came nearer and, leaning forward a little, looked into my eyes.

'Blue eyes—I trust them. But don't trust green eyes. And yellow eyes are evil.'

'I've never seen yellow eyes.'

'That's because you're pure,' she said, and turned away and hurried across the lawn as though she had just remembered a very urgent appointment.

The sun was up, slanting through the branches of the banyan tree, and Ayah's voice could be heard calling me for breakfast.

'Dukhi,' I said, when I found him in the garden later that day, 'Dukhi, don't kill the snake in the banyan tree.'

'A snake in the banyan tree!' he exclaimed, seizing his hose.

'No, no!' I said. 'I haven't seen it. But the Rani says there's one. She says it was a prince in its former life, and that we shouldn't kill it.'

'Oh,' said Dukhi, smiling to himself. 'The Rani says so. All right, you tell her we won't kill it.'

'Is it true that she was in love with a prince but that he died before she could marry him?'

'Something like that,' said Dukhi. 'It was a long time ago—before I came here.'

'My father says it wasn't a prince, but a commoner. Are you a commoner, Dukhi?'

'A commoner? What's that, Chota Sahib?'

'I'm not sure. Someone very poor, I suppose.'

'Then I must be a commoner,' said Dukhi.

'Were you in love with the Rani?' I asked.

Dukhi was so startled that he dropped his hose and lost his balance; the first time I'd seen him lose his poise while squatting on his haunches.

'Don't say such things, Chota Sahib!'

'Why not?'

'You'll get me into trouble.'

'Then it must be true.'

Dukhi threw up his hands in mock despair and started collecting his implements.

'It's true, it's true!' I cried, dancing round him, and then I ran indoors to Ayah and said, 'Ayah, Dukhi was in love with the Rani!'

Ayah gave a shriek of laughter, then looked very serious and put her finger against my lips.

'Don't say such things,' she said. 'Dukhi is of a very low caste. People won't like it if they hear what you say. And besides, the Rani told you her prince died and turned into a snake. Well, Dukhi hasn't become a snake as yet, has he?'

True, Dukhi didn't look as though he could be anything but a gardener; but I wasn't satisfied with his denials or with Ayah's attempts to still my tongue. Hadn't Dukhi sent the Rani a nosegay?

When my father came home, he looked quite pleased with himself.

'What have you brought for me?' was the first question I asked.

He had brought me some new books, a dartboard, and a train set; and in my excitement over examining these gifts, I forgot to ask about the result of his trip.

It was during tiffin that he told me what had happened—and what was going to happen.

'We'll be going away soon,' he said. 'I've joined the Royal Air Force. I'll have to work in Delhi.'

'Oh! Will you be in the war, Dad? Will you fly a plane?'

'No, I'm too old to be flying planes. I'll be forty years old in July. The RAF will be giving me what they call intelligence work—decoding secret messages and things like that and I don't suppose I'll be able to tell you much about it.'

This didn't sound as exciting as flying planes, but it sounded important and rather mysterious.

'Well, I hope it's interesting,' I said. 'Is Delhi a good place to live in?'

'I'm not sure. It will be very hot by the middle of April. And you won't be able to stay with me, Ruskin—not at first, anyway, not until I can get married quarters and then, only if your mother returns... Meanwhile, you'll stay with your grandmother in Dehra.' He must have seen the disappointment in my face, because he quickly added: 'Of course, I'll come to see you often. Dehra isn't far from Delhi—only a night's train journey.'

But I was dismayed. It wasn't that I didn't want to stay with my grandmother, but I had grown so used to sharing my father's life and even watching him at work, that the thought of being separated from him was unbearable.

'Not as bad as going to boarding school,' he said. 'And that's the only alternative.'

'Not boarding school,' I said quickly, 'I'll run away from boarding school.'

'Well, you won't want to run away from your grandmother. She's very fond of you. And if you come with me to Delhi, you'll be alone all day in a stuffy little hut while I'm away at work. Sometimes I may have to go on tour—then what happens?'

'I don't mind being on my own.' And this was true. I had already grown accustomed to having my own room and my own trunk and my own bookshelf and I felt as though I was about to lose these things.

'Will Ayah come too?' I asked.

My father looked thoughtful. 'Would you like that?'

'Ayah must come,' I said firmly. 'Otherwise I'll run away.'

'I'll have to ask her,' said my father.

Ayah, it turned out, was quite ready to come with us. In fact, she was indignant that Father should have considered leaving her behind. She had brought me up since my mother went away, and she wasn't going to hand over charge to any upstart aunt or governess. She was pleased and excited at the prospect of the move, and this helped to raise my spirits.

'What is Dehra like?' I asked my father.

'It's a green place,' he said. 'It lies in a valley in the foothills of the Himalayas, and it's surrounded by forests. There are lots of trees in Dehra.'

'Does Grandmother's house have trees?'

'Yes. There's a big jackfruit tree in the garden. Your grandmother planted it when I was a boy. And there's an old banyan tree, which is good to climb. And there are fruit trees, litchis, mangoes, papayas.'

'Are there any books?'

'Grandmother's books won't interest you. But I'll be bringing you books from Delhi whenever I come to see you.'

I was beginning to look forward to the move. Changing houses had always been fun. Changing towns ought to be fun, too.

A few days before we left, I went to say goodbye to the Rani.

'I'm going away,' I said.

'How lovely!' said the Rani. 'I wish I could go away!'

'Why don't you?'

'They won't let me. They're afraid to let me out of the palace.'

'What are they afraid of, Your Highness?'

'That I might run away. Run away, far, far away, to the land where the leopards are learning to pray.'

Gosh, I thought, she's really quite crazy... But then she was silent, and started smoking a small hookah.

She drew on the hookah, looked at me, and asked, 'Where is your mother?'

'I haven't one.'

'Everyone has a mother. Did yours die?'

'No. She went away.'

She drew on her hookah again and then said, very sweetly, 'Don't go away...'

'I must,' I said. 'It's because of the war.'

'What war? Is there a war on? You see, no one tells me anything.'

'It's between us and Hitler,' I said.

'And who is Hitler?'

'He's a German.'

'I knew a German once, Dr Schreinherr, he had beautiful hands.'

'Was he an artist?'

'He was a dentist.'

The Rani got up from her couch and accompanied me out on to the balcony. When we looked down at the garden, we could see Dukhi weeding a flower bed. Both of us gazed down at him in silence, and I wondered what the Rani would say if I asked her if she had ever been in love with the palace gardener. Ayah had told me it would be an insulting question, so I held my peace. But as I walked slowly down the spiral staircase, the Rani's voice came after me.

'Thank him,' she said. 'Thank him for the beautiful rose.'

THE CORAL TREE

The night had been hot, the rain frequent, and I slept on the verandah instead of in the house. I was in my twenties and I had begun to earn a living and felt I had certain responsibilities. In a short while a tonga would take me to a railway station, and from there a train would take me to Bombay, and then a ship would take me to England. There would be work, interviews, a job, a different kind of life; so many things that this small bungalow of my grandfather's would be remembered fitfully, in rare moments of reflection.

When I awoke on the verandah I saw a grey morning, smelt the rain on the red earth, and remembered that I had to go away. A girl was standing on the verandah porch, looking at me very seriously. When I saw her, I sat up in bed with a start.

She was a small, dark girl, her eyes big and black, her pigtails tied up in a bright red ribbon; and she was fresh and clean like the rain and the red earth.

She stood looking at me, and she was very serious.

'Hello,' I said, smiling, trying to put her at ease.

But the girl was businesslike. She acknowledged my greeting with a brief nod.

'Can I do anything for you?' I asked, stretching my limbs. 'Do you stay near here?'

She nodded again.

'With your parents?'

With great assurance she said, 'Yes. But I can stay on my own.'

'You're like me,' I said, and for a while I forgot about being an old man of twenty. 'I like to do things on my own. I'm going away today.'

'Oh,' she said, a little breathlessly.

'Would you care to go to England?'

'I want to go everywhere,' she said, 'to America and Africa and Japan and Honolulu.'

'Maybe you will,' I said. 'I'm going everywhere, and no one can stop me... But what is it you want? What did you come for?'

'I want some flowers but I can't reach them.' She waved her hand towards the garden. 'That tree, see?'

The coral tree stood in front of the house surrounded by pools of water and broken, fallen blossoms. The branches of the tree were thick with the scarlet, pea-shaped flowers.

'All right,' I said. 'Just let me get ready.'

The tree was easy to climb, and I made myself comfortable on one of the lower branches, smiling down at the serious upturned face of the girl.

'I'll throw them down to you,' I said.

I bent a branch but the wood was young and green, and I had to twist it several times before it snapped.

'I'm not sure that I ought to do this,' I said, as I dropped the flowering branch to the girl.

'Don't worry,' she said.

'Well, if you're ready to speak up for me—'

'Don't worry.'

I felt a sudden nostalgic longing for childhood and an urge to remain behind in my grandfather's house with its tangled memories and ghosts of yesteryear. But I was the only one left, and what could I do except climb coral and jackfruit trees?

'Have you many friends?' I asked.

'Oh, yes.'

'Who is the best?'

'The cook. He lets me stay in the kitchen, which is more interesting than the house. And I like to watch him cooking. And he gives me things to eat, and tells me stories...'

'And who is your second best friend?'

She inclined her head to one side, and thought very hard.

'I'll make you the second best,' she said.

I sprinkled coral blossoms over her head. 'That's very kind of you. I'm happy to be your second best.'

A tonga bell sounded at the gate, and I looked out from the tree and said, 'It's come for me. I have to go now.'

I climbed down.

'Will you help me with my suitcases?' I asked, as we walked together towards the verandah. 'There is no one here to help me. I am the last to go. Not because I want to go, but because I have to.'

I sat down on the cot and packed a few last things in a suitcase. All the doors of the house were locked. On my way to the station I would leave the keys with the caretaker. I had already given instructions to an agent to try and sell the house. There was nothing more to be done.

We walked in silence to the waiting tonga, thinking and

wondering about each other.

'Take me to the station,' I said to the tonga driver.

The girl stood at the side of the path, on the damp red earth, gazing at me.

'Thank you,' I Mid. 'I hope I shall see you again.'

'I'll see you in London,' she said, 'or America or Japan. I want to go everywhere.'

'I'm sure you will,' I said. 'And perhaps I'll come back and we'll meet again in this garden. That would be nice, wouldn't it?'

She nodded and smiled. We knew it was an important moment.

The tonga driver spoke to his pony, and the carriage set off down the gravel path, rattling a little. The girl and I waved to each other.

In the girl's hand was a sprig of coral blossom. As she waved, the blossoms fell apart and danced lightly in the breeze.

'Goodbye!' I called.

'Goodbye!' called the girl.

The ribbon had come loose from her pigtail and lay on the ground with the coral blossoms.

'I'm going everywhere,' I said to myself, 'and no one can stop me'.

And she was fresh and clean like the rain and the red earth.